PRAISE FOR
A PALACE NEAR THE WIND

"Enchanting, mysterious, and strange, *A Palace Near the Wind* is a heartbreaking story of homecoming and self-discovery. Combining the best of folklore and science fiction, this eco-narrative on human greed and superhuman hope is not to be missed."

KRITIKA H. RAO, author of *The Surviving Sky*

"A fantastic and magical tale of survival and rebellion set against the backdrop of a struggle between nature and the forces of industry. Ai Jiang has written a beautiful and all-too-fitting story that resonates with the choices we face in our times."

P. DJÈLÍ CLARK, author of *The Dead Cat Tail Assassins* and *A Master of Djinn*

"A breathtakingly imagined story of ecological disaster, torn families, betrayal, and hope. Unlike anything I've ever read before—like Ghibli retelling Tolkien through Chinese myth—with tree-like deities, political intrigue, wind magic, and mecha. Utterly enchanting."

A.Y. CHAO, author of *Shanghai Immortal*

"Beautifully written and intricately layered, this novella is part fairy tale and part tale of rebellion and hope. A compelling and complex story of court politics, hidden secrets, sacrifices, alliances, and characters fighting for their freedom."

A.C. WISE, author of *Wendy, Darling* and *Hooked*

"Haunting and lovely, Jiang creates a world of wonder in *A Palace Near the Wind*. Your heart will break as Lufeng must give up her home, her beliefs, and her sense of family. You'll root for her as she builds her courage to forge a new future for herself, and those precious to her."

JULIA VEE, co-author of The Phoenix Hoard trilogy

"Elegant and otherworldly. A tale of family and duty, devotion and obligation—and the shattering secrets hidden in every past. A glorious new myth from a talented new voice."

A.G. SLATTER, author of *All the Murmuring Bones* and *The Briar Book of the Dead*

Coming soon from Ai Jiang and Titan Books

A River from the Sky

A PALACE NEAR the WIND

AI JIANG

TITAN BOOKS

A Palace Near the Wind
Print edition ISBN: 9781803369389
Signed edition ISBN: 9781835414736
Inkstone edition ISBN: 9781835414330
Broken Binding edition ISBN: 9781835414729
E-book edition ISBN: 9781803369396

Published by Titan Books
A division of Titan Publishing Group Ltd
144 Southwark Street, London SE1 0UP
www.titanbooks.com

First edition: April 2025
10 9 8 7 6 5 4 3 2 1

A CIP catalogue record for this title is available from the British Library.

EU RP
eucomply OÜ Pärnu mnt 139b-14 11317
Tallinn, Estonia
hello@eucompliancepartner.com
+3375690241

Printed and bound by CPI Group (UK) Ltd, Croydon, CR0 4YY.

*For Mother Nature and all
her unwilling sacrifices.*

BRIDEWEALTH

C huiliu blew on the white and blue rain blooms as she clutched tight their navy stems. The dozens of slender arms protruding from their tips held onto teardrop-like bulbs. Her breath scattered the seeds so they may travel and grow elsewhere.

One ancient story passed down in Feng told of the floating seeds helping those who blew them to find what they were seeking. There was little doubt my sister and I were praying for the same thing: to find our sisters and mother. We denied the possibility of their death for the annuals they had spent, sight unseen, within the Palace. Grandmother would've told us. We would've held a funeral.

All we held now was our silence and uncertainty.

Even with sunlight beckoning the forest to stretch its limbs and drink its rays, the warmth was not comforting.

It battered and scorched my body, igniting the pent-up anger and sorrow within.

A sob welled at the thought of my three younger sisters and mother when they were still in Feng. Back then, it felt as though our home was in an eternal spring. At dusk, in the rain-bloom fields, Yunshu, Heshi, Sangshu, and I offered whispers of our dreams of love, of age, of adventure. Mother always watched, settled under a nearby storm tree, with a gentle smile reaching her eyes. It had been three annuals since second-youngest sister Sangshu married the King. She'd be twenty-three annuals if she was alive. She is. Or so I told myself.

Chuiliu was unaware of my sorrow as I shielded my face from her, not wanting my youngest sister to watch as I crumbled. I imagined the rain-bloom droplets lifting into the sky with my own sap tears.

"Will the seeds find them?" Chuiliu's eyes were like earthy moons.

"The natural gods and the wind will guide them." A lie.

I, too, would soon be married to the King. I couldn't tell her I would act as her seeking rain bloom. All she had to do was wait for my return.

"Lufeng," Grandmother's voice drifted from behind. "It is time."

I patted Chuiliu's head, her dark needle threads soft against the rough bark of my skin, and nudged her towards the cluster of hollows making up our home in Feng. Reluctant at first, her shoulders then drooped before she trotted away. Grandmother and I waited until she disappeared into the storm trees' embrace.

Two individuals must settle the negotiation of bridewealth; they must be close—yet not too close—to the soon-to-be-married couple's families.

This was the first time marriage negotiations were taking place in Feng.

My mother's sister, Xiangmu, and Copper, the King's aunt, would meet to negotiate the terms of my marriage to the King. The Palace grounds tore forth again, growing ever closer to our home. Only through the marriages would there be a chance to halt—or at least delay—the relentless expansions.

I followed Grandmother away from the fields towards the edge of Feng and waited for Copper to exit the Palace. We stood obscured by large storm-tree leaves, grey, shifting, like a slice of dark sky and clouds contained within the naturally serrated edges. Driven by slivers of wind, the tree brewed small hurricanes and tornadoes, a flurry of branches and trunks intertwining. Yet, only soft tickles graced our fingertips when we brushed the storm leaves aside, like collected dust, touchable clouds, soft tumbleweeds.

The gates of the Palace yawned like the opening of a freshly dug grave. Settled on top of a bulky and imposing

Traveler, Copper towered over both the Palace guards, whose machines were half the height of hers. They flanked Copper both ahead and behind, adorned in pooling black cloaks with the hoods drawn up, hanging just before the lips. The controlled strides of the Travelers' mechanical legs creaked metallically, resounding between the Palace and Feng. Copper and the Palace guards moved forth in a rhythm, too steady, on their Travelers, with silver legs, feet, and talons resembling those of birds.

The Palace was too far—an hour away by wind, far less on a Traveler—for the eyes and ears of those who lived within the Palace, Land Wanderers. But the sound met us early. The same with sight. Even Grandmother, ancient in her age, could see every detail of a single feather on a bird's wing several gusts of winds away. I had heard Land Wanderers had no such capabilities.

The walls extending skywards around the Palace grazed the clouds. The Palace itself seemed encased in a bone mold—rigid, still… dead. Few had seen past the walls. Along the bottom, there were more waiting tiles, stacked on top of uprooted trees and dead undergrowth like feeble fingers, clutching, scraping, futile.

If I had the power, if the wind ever allowed—though I knew the natural gods were never in favor of chaos— I would show the King what it was like to have his home threatened, to feel attacked, to be afraid. And I would mock his terror in silence.

A PALACE NEAR THE WIND

At the abrupt end of the bone-tiled path stretching forth with the width of a large forest stream, the three halted in unison halfway to Feng. The guards retreated. Copper continued forth alone. Her smooth, bronzed skin and slender arms were so unlike our own rough bark faces and carved branch limbs. Her white cloak billowed; her hood framed her face. I winced when the metal talons of her Traveler sank into the grass, uprooting with each step, leaving scars, marring our lands.

When Copper neared, seemingly only moments later, though the sun had already gone, I melted into the shadows and trailed behind—unseen and unheard—as she made for Aunt Xiangmu's home near the heart of Feng.

The Wind Walkers exited their hollows and watched with bowed heads as the King's aunt passed. Some marveled at the Traveler; some stared with scorn; a few withdrew into their homes, the sight too horrific; while others stood, feet bracing both the earth beneath them and the wind hovering near them—sometimes we borrowed for travel, and other times we borrowed for strength.

Each step Copper's Traveler took pierced into the organs of Feng. I reimagined the ground as Copper, the Traveler's legs as my fingers, and the King as the soil crumbling beneath the talons.

Near the entrance of Aunt Xiangmu's home sat Copper's Traveler, legs withdrawn, the half-shell body settled on the ground. Without her machine, Copper's height was swallowed by the hollow's intertwined roots reaching endlessly upwards, roofless. Beneath, branches wormed down into the earth, rippling. Storm vines hung from leaning hollow trunks, making it almost impossible to see inside—almost. The woven branch walls rippled every few seconds, allowing small glimpses into the earthy chamber, now an intruded-upon haven. I liked to call these homes eyes for the way they blinked.

I crouched on the other side of a shifting opening, caught a rippling, and tugged it to widen the gap.

During prior negotiations, Aunt Xiangmu would glide as if on clouds towards the Palace, guided by the wind, while my sisters, Grandmother, and I bid her a silent farewell half-hidden behind the walls of Feng—tangled, spiraling in place like churning clouds, rumbling storms. Perhaps this slight change, bringing a member of the Palace to us, meant we were making progress in reclaiming our lands. Or perhaps the King was only toying with us—giving us false hope before taking it away.

Chuiliu tugged at my cloak. Even at full height, she only reached my hip, and I was shorter than most from Feng, only past five feet, halfway to six. "Fengfeng."

The Feng—*Phoenix*—in my name was not the same

meaning as the Feng, *Wind*, of our home, but my youngest sister, still having difficulties with the distinct tones, always made the same mistake.

"Feng—" I raised a finger to my lips and beckoned her closer as I leaned down towards her. Though Chuiliu was naturally quiet, her whispers sounded thunderous with only the wind against the grass and a single cricket's call.

She lowered her voice until it was almost inaudible. "What are you doing?"

"Watching. Listening." I wrapped my arms around her slight frame and brought her to a squat, our limbs of braided and tangled branches blending with the hollow. The only thing distinguishing our legs from one another was the newness of her roots: no moss, loose, as though they would unravel with a strong passing breeze.

I clutched Chuiliu's hand harder than she was clutching mine. In an unexpected gesture, she reached behind me, offering rhythmic pats the same way Mother used to soothe us all. Though she was the youngest, often her maturity surprised me.

Together, we watched the negotiations unfold.

Aunt Xiangmu sat across from Copper in her dinner hollow, one that remained empty elsetime, with hands settled on top of a scarred table made from the remains of our ancestors, their faces lit by a single candle Copper had brought with her, now almost burnt out. I winced as drops of melted wax met the table, as if burning our dead.

Each aunt had an emptied shell filled with tea made from riverside herbs. We didn't need such things, but we understood Land Wanderers required different nourishment. Water, soil, sunlight, and moonlight were enough to sustain us. Land Wanderers were always picky, according to Aunt Xiangmu. Yet my younger sisters were always eager, hungry, to hear more about the Palace and its people. *There's nothing better than our home*, I used to remind them, as Grandmother would me. My sisters would sulk and return to playing in the rain-bloom fields, or sometimes past those, swinging or crawling through vineyard thickets.

Copper pulled a second candle from her white cloak.

In Feng, we only borrowed Moonglows, tiny insects carrying the moon's light in their bodies, and we always allowed them to leave when they wished. We didn't need the light for our eyesight adjusted to the time of moon. Moonglows were mainly for company, comfort, celebration. Yunshu and Heshi had a habit of beckoning Moonglows into their hairs, complimenting one another on the beauty of their needle threads. Chuiliu liked to stare in silence, wordless, at the Moonglows with a small grin.

But there was also a different type of Moonglow with

the same name, which grew where their crescents hung in trees, a slow juggle across the sky. For those of us injured or nearing death, Moonglows were ground, mixed, poured down throats, churned within ourselves to heal, to purify. It felt like the dim recollection of the sun at dawn, a small embrace during the nights. And sometimes, it was used for tea.

"Thank you," Aunt Xiangmu began in Script, the tongue of Land Wanderers, gesturing to the tea in front of Copper. "For coming all the way here."

It was a strange clang and clink of words, grinding together like gears. Even though we knew Script too—the bare minimum—most of us had no reason to use it unless we encountered Palace folk. I'd known no other spoken tongue than that of the wind—Breath, like rhythmic leavings of air from our lungs to shape the words we spoke—until I turned twenty a few annuals prior.

"Well, the King wanted to extend his respects to the Wind Walkers. The situation has been uneasy between our people, hasn't it?" Copper took a sip, wrinkled her nose. "It's cold."

"Is it not to your liking?" Aunt Xiangmu took a sip of her own tea, unfazed.

Copper pressed her lips together. "No, no. Just… different." The movement was slight, but when Copper placed her shell down, she slid it away.

I held my tongue. I wondered if Aunt Xiangmu had drunk the hot tea she once spoke about being served at the Palace and had served Copper cold tea as an act of unspoken defiance. The thought brought a small smile to my face.

"Hopefully, with this meeting, your people will become more"—Copper tapped a finger against the side of the shell—"settled with their concerns."

"That will depend on whether you agree to our terms." Aunt Xiangmu set down her tea, fingers tightening around the shell.

"Surely, you understand your people are at a disadvantage." Copper thumbed her three bone rings. I imagined their texture as both grainy and smooth, like sanded teeth—like the tiles stretching in all directions from the Palace.

Copper swept her white hair aside, her face too youthful in contrast, revealing bone earrings, hanging in the shape of loosely connected joints.

"With the Palace expanding, what could you possibly have left to offer? The King was quite," Copper sniffed, "disappointed with the last one." She brought a finger up to her lip. "She didn't seem to embrace Palace life, unlike the others—well, and the mother, of course."

The others—mother—could that mean—? Hope swelled within me, but I dared not allow it to grow too rampant, to only later have it snuffed out.

Copper bowed, eyes set on Aunt Xiangmu with a calculating stare—an attempt to provoke—yet there was also a flicker of something else, an unspoken exchange between Copper and Aunt Xiangmu I couldn't decipher. And for a moment too quick for me to be certain of, it was as though Copper had looked right where Chuiliu and I were hiding.

During the last negotiation discussions between Aunt Xiangmu and Grandmother, I overheard I was to be last. My sisters and I had been born one annual after another, but Chuiliu was unplanned. I was glad for Chuiliu's age, her youthfulness making her ineligible for a sacrificial marriage—at least for now. I drew her closer. She tilted her head, resting against me. Her innocence, her unawareness, made me want to never let go.

"This one's aware of her duties," Aunt Xiangmu said. I shivered at the way she referenced me, like an object rather than a living being.

"Oh, is she?" Copper looked amused.

Aunt Xiangmu understood Copper would propose outrageous requests. They were ignorant to the death they brought with their pavings, what they called "development" and "construction." Such faithless Land Wanderers who reviled Feng's natural gods. For my mother, they halted the expansions towards Feng for five annuals, and the offers had been decreasing with each sister.

"Who do we have the honor of welcoming to the Palace this time?" Copper cooed.

"The eldest granddaughter of our Elder," Aunt Xiangmu said. "Lufeng."

The resolution in my aunt's voice caused all of me to constrict and curl, the bark of my limbs prying. Aunt Xiangmu interlaced her hands with a slight tremor.

"Lufeng. *Green* Phoenix. How fascinating," Copper said. "The juxtaposition between a creature of flames and the color of vitality. Truly, the people of Feng have such a gift for names. But," her smile was wicked, "maybe she, too, will change hers, like her sisters."

I immediately expelled the thought of my sisters abandoning their identities from my mind. They were loyal to Feng. They wouldn't do such a thing of their own volition. The King must have forced the betrayal.

"So, what is it the Feng desire?" Copper drawled.

Aunt's transpiring palms gripped her grass skirt, crushing the floral decorations. A cold breeze uncharacteristic of Feng's usual warmth caused the skin of my limbs to contract, branches tightening, the crevices across my face sealing.

"We want cessation of construction in Eastern Feng and the nearby plains. And removal of the new Palace ground pavings from the annual prior." Then, after a pause, Aunt Xiangmu said, "Permanently."

Copper tsked. "*Well*. That is *quite* the ask. Is she so special?" Copper's amusement drew up her painted lips.

"Lufeng is the eldest. The next in line to lead the people of Feng after the Elder," Aunt Xiangmu said.

No doubt Copper saw the risks Feng was taking and the opportunities for the Palace's further growth: their trade ventures, new markets, more roads. To weaken our hold on Feng and its lands, its resources—

"You know we cannot agree to a permanent stop to the construction, the *progress*. We must move forward, even if slowly." Copper was thoughtful. "A decade. Would that suffice?"

When Aunt Xiangmu didn't respond, Copper frowned, and there was a twitch to her eye. "This is already a more than generous offer."

Aunt Xiangmu's expression soured, but she quickly smoothed the crease on her forehead and lifted the downwards turn of her lips. For a long pause, she considered the proposition—a show. Then her shoulders sagged with defeat.

Copper crossed her legs, smiling. Her rows of too-straight teeth, bone white, shone in the dimming candlelight. There was silence as the two blew out the quivering flame, each pressing a slit finger—a smear of blood from Copper, glistening sap from Aunt Xiangmu— onto the agreement. The sight of the parchment made me shudder. I thought of all the dead trees, our unspeaking kin, and I mourned them in silence.

The wedding would take place in a cycle's time.

When Copper had left and Aunt Xiangmu had rid her hollow of the unnatural candle and tea, and had withdrawn for sleep, Chuiliu squirmed out of my hold.

She stood, fists clenched at her side with what strength and anger and fear she could muster. "You can't leave!" Sap tears dribbled down her chin.

"I don't want to, but I must." I ran the edge of my cloak along her jawline, collecting escaped pain.

Chuiliu didn't yet understand the sacrifices necessary to keep our lands. I stroked her unruly, dirt-speckled needle threads.

The only thing we could do was continue resisting. If we could come to understand them, perhaps they would come to understand us. That was my mother and grandmother's wish. I had little choice but to honor them, even if I disagreed. We could only hold the King back for so long.

The storm trees behind us shifted in tortured twists. If the natural gods could hear me, I questioned why they continued to make us sacrifice.

Grandmother appeared from the trees. She approached, slow, then rested a hand on my shoulder. I never knew where she disappeared to, or how she knew when she was needed, but rather than feeling comfort, I felt the weight of her position, the weight of Feng, and the weight of her faith.

Mother believed there could be peace. She believed the King would understand why a balance between the new world and the natural world was necessary. She was wrong. I may well be another futile sacrifice. I didn't voice this to anyone. It was not my place to. I would have to take the risk no one else had taken, or at least no one had succeeded in taking.

I would have to kill the King—

Even if it meant imprisonment.

Even if it meant exile.

Even if it meant execution

FENG

At sunrise, a quarter cycle after the bridewealth negotiations, Grandmother and I headed towards the rain grasslands beside the forests of Eastern Feng. Ten steam engines several times my height with wheels as thick as five ancient trunks bound together littered the space, their weight crushing the sparse remains of the land. I couldn't help but imagine how easily I would be pulped beneath these monstrous entities, the way slender twigs snapped under Land Wanderers' feet.

There were piles upon piles of uprooted plants scattered across almost barren land. Toppled trees, too many to count, had their branches sprawled over one another—broken limbs, fallen bodies, cooling corpses. It was difficult to picture the space as once lush with towering rain grass that hid roaming creatures.

I dropped next to a young storm tree still standing, its trunk the size of my forearm, the leaves on its severed branches already wilted. My throat clenched at the sight of fur clumps—grey, brown, white—among flattened foliage. Only bones and tuffs remained.

"Stop!" Grandmother commanded the builders, her voice drowned out by the destruction roaming around us, a stark contrast to the whispering winds rustling through the trees of Feng. She waved the scroll containing the bridewealth agreement in the air. "We have negotiated the bridewealth with the King."

The chief builder half-strolled, half-swayed towards her and swiped the parchment. An uncle who used to live near our hollow in Feng. The trichomes along my limbs bristled and straightened in defiance. The chief builder took his time unrolling the scroll, scanning its contents slowly, though it was not more than a page, then he nodded. I glimpsed a drawn map, marked in red and black. The chief turned to his fellow workers.

"Remove the Ground Turners and bring them westward." His chin, once sporting a long beard, was now shaven. "You can't keep this up forever, Elder."

Grandmother straightened. "We can, and we will."

The chief shook his head, his bright red helmet bobbing. "This is innovation. This is the future. You can't remain in the past."

"We are trying to save our future."

The chief rubbed at a grease stain on his orange overalls, strange clothing nonexistent in Feng. Outside of our cloaks, we wore no clothes at all unless for a specific occasion, such as when those like Copper visited from the Palace.

Hope welled within me as Grandmother took a step towards the chief. Though she was half the height, she seemed much taller. The chief offered one last skeptical glance before backing away, propelling himself onto his Traveler. Its mechanical legs squealed, its creaking not unlike the sound of saws slicing through wooden flesh, causing me to grit my teeth, my bark tightening uncomfortably. It was older, rusted, compared to the ones Copper and the Palace guards rode, and smaller. Yet at two times my height, it loomed like an awaiting predator.

"You should get one," the chief patted the side of his Traveler. "The world is advancing. You're all going to be left behind."

"We have the wind."

In the past, the wind was good enough for the chief as well. It seemed the Land Wanderers had convinced him otherwise. Sorrow brewed within me at the thought of him giving up something so beautiful and wondrous for this grotesque and unnatural creation.

The builder shook his head once more before leaving the two of us among rubble and damaged soil, along with the corpses of trees and plants that had clung onto one another in their last moments. I immortalized the tragic image of their desperate embrace before the builders crushed their remains.

Some of the guards and builders were once our neighbors, distant family, friends, but settled on top of Travelers and the Ground Turners, they looked like strangers. Perhaps Father had chosen the same path. No one really spoke about him in Feng, and whenever I asked Grandmother, she'd simply say he was dead.

"Call the healers," Grandmother whispered. "Our land has fallen ill." The healers could speed up the growth of new life and repair the damage caused by the Ground Turners. I sent a message through the wind.

I allowed the wind to carry me back towards Feng where the healers were already gathering as though they had heard their land's silent weeping. Without words, the land spoke to them, just like the wind spoke to all of us. But the life of a healer was short. Each time they healed, they stepped closer to death.

Grandmother and I watched our people leave Feng one by one, following the promises of the Palace—some with woven sacks thrown across their backs, others with nothing but the earthy cloaks of Feng. I couldn't remember when or why we began wearing cloaks. It was long before I was born, but with the bareness of the surrounding trees, I couldn't believe the cloaks were an aesthetic choice.

In a scattered line, the leavers walked towards the Palace. Copper and the King had sent Travelers for those who requested them. Though not many asked, the sight of our people on these strange machines unsettled me, like seeing the chief had; the memory of him walking on the wind replaced with the jarring sight of creaky limbs, leaving footprints that the wind never would. As they treaded from our home, I could feel the wind mourning being left behind.

One merchant turned. "There's more outside of Feng. More to discover." Their expression was one of pity.

Fury welled up within me, but I couldn't help but linger on their words and their truth. My entire life in Feng had consisted of being told what to do, what to think, how to act, who to be—Yunshu and Heshi had often mocked me, saying I was simply Grandmother's puppet, a shadow. I wondered if Sangshu thought the same. I wasn't the role model they wanted—needed, perhaps—and I may never be.

As the merchant backed away, I threw out a hand, but Grandmother raised an arm over my chest, untouching.

"We have to stop them!" Desperation's cruel fingers dug into me.

Grandmother hummed. "It is their choice."

"But what if they're wrong? What if they regret it? It's our duty—"

A throaty croak left her lips, and to my surprise, a

grin deepened her age lines. "Yes, it is our duty to protect them, but it is not our duty to make their decisions for them."

We watched as the leavers trudged on bare feet, almost sluggish without the wind. They moved in pairs, sometimes in groups, and sometimes alone.

"For them, the Travelers are their wind and their rivers."

"But the wind and river will always be here, in one form or another, as long as the gods. Those contraptions may break down," I said. Yet, even as the words left me, I wondered how true that was as I eyed how far the Palace had reached with its tiles.

"Yes, as long as the gods..." Grandmother agreed with a strange melancholy to her tone that confused me.

At the graves of Feng, where the Memory Clouds clustered, I wrung my hands together then clutched at Grandmother's jade ring around my neck, slick with transpiration, its pale surface matching the earthy tones of my eyes.

Soon, I'd have to leave the familiarity of the wood chips of my bed, the gentle caressing breezes, and the squirrel that often nestled on my lap.

"Lufeng." Grandmother drew closer when she called a second time, though the echo from her first call still hung in the air.

I pushed aside the swaying leaves, translucent, resembling a mixture of raw cotton and webs spun by spiders, and finished carving my likeness onto the bark of a Memory Cloud. Above it sat the portraits of my three sisters, and above that was my mother's, Gaiwang—the *gai* in 'change' and *wang* in 'hope'. I traced the carvings surrounded by soft moss. Written language was unused in Feng outside of names.

I am coming.

"I'm ready," I said, more to myself than to Grandmother.

Grandmother approached and handed me a thin necklace woven using lightning twigs, zigzagged, as though collected directly from a storm. I let the ring drop between my collarbones and fastened it around my neck. Her outstretched hand settled over the ring.

"Remember where you come from," she echoed the words she had said to each of my sisters before me.

We are the people of Feng and Feng itself—a part of the trees, a part of the wind. Just as we borrow the wind, the wind also borrows us.

I bowed, committing her past and present words to memory.

When Grandmother left me, Chuiliu stepped out from her hiding place a few paces away.

"When will you come back?" She stared, wide-eyed, fingers twitching at the frayed edges of my cloak. Though she had little command over the wind at her age, it always seemed to surround her, carrying her long needle threads upwards, waiting for her to borrow. Chuiliu would be powerful when she became older—perhaps even greater than Grandmother. I didn't want her to end up like the rest of us.

"Soon," I tried to convince myself. "Soon."

3

THE PALACE

A quarter cycle passed before I stood, curved branch-like toes, used to digging into soft soil, now refusing to touch the tiles that stretched halfway to Feng. Their surfaces were shaved down too finely. I clung onto the wind to keep me afloat. Behind me the switch grass—wild, unruly, but free—ended, trimmed to a straight edge.

The walls of the Palace shimmered in the sunlight—made from the bones of squirrels and deer and rabbits, polished after the meat had been stripped off their bodies and consumed by the Land Wanderers like savages. Most of the windows—closed—were made of slatted metal. A shudder ran through my body as I imagined the sound of squealing metal against bone. The surface of the metallic double doors held engravings of Travelers, Ground Turners, and other unknown contraptions.

At their center, there was a large bird with no eyes, the lines of its body too sharp.

To think humans couldn't see the distances we could, the weakness of their naked eyes, baffled me. Perhaps that was why they couldn't survive in nature and must hide in palaces, why they couldn't sense danger until it was far too late. Perhaps that was also why they had so many contraptions.

My hood fluttered, allowing the wind to whip dark tendrils into my face. At the edge of Feng, next to Grandmother, Chuiliu's shadow quivered like the static of lightning behind clouds. Feng seemed so small, the trees like ants compared to the towering bone mass.

The doors of the Palace opened and the King emerged. Though I had not seen him before, I had no doubt. Perhaps it was the ominous air he gave about him, and yet there was also a slight vulnerability masterfully veiled.

His white-cloaked head loomed over the guards—a giant even next to the Travelers. Only his pointed chin and lips were visible. A flash of a smile revealed the same unnaturally straight teeth as Copper's—both charming and unsettling.

Two guards marched towards me, like small chicks in the distance. Their chain mail peeked from under their cloaks, clinking against the Travelers atop which they sat. Grey hoods obscured the top half of their faces, exposing only unsmiling mouths. A sterile scent emitted from the guards as they neared me, driving away the musky moss I was accustomed to. There was an unnerving similarity between the guards, a twin-like symmetry in both movement and appearance.

"Welcome." The King's voice, low, echoed when the guards reached me, as though it came from the sky, and simultaneously caressed my ears—an intimate vibration against the drums within—rising the fine trichomes around them. I wanted nothing more than to dispel the invasive tingle it left. There was surely a hidden machine amplifying his voice. I'd only experienced such a device used once, by a builder to command his workers.

Our eyes locked when the King looked up, revealing a glint from the shift of his hood—my earthy jade challenging his silver. The same razor-edged smile from before slid across his ageless face, but there was a strange vulnerability and youth behind the coldness, one reminding me of Chuiliu, and one also reminding me of Mother. I bit my tongue, tasted sap.

My heels peeled off the tiles as I took careful steps past the guards. Activated Cleaners trailing behind me quickly swept the traces of soil that loosened from the creases of my feet. My presence was the only thing marring the path's spotless perfection.

When I finally reached the entrance, the King was nowhere to be found.

The booming echoes of the Palace doors as they closed behind me. Stale quiet assaulted my ears. There was no rustling grass, sighing trees, or murmuring creatures. The guards dismounted their Travelers, escorting me to my room.

The wedding would be in half a cycle. They insisted I stay within my sleeping chamber at night, but I was welcome to roam the grounds of the Palace during the day. From their stilted and stiff Script tone, it was obvious they were not native to the Palace.

To me, the Palace was a sinister entity. Yunshu and Heshi had thought it was marvelous, drawn in by its eerie beauty, and often moondreamed about exploring its corridors. And yet, now that I was walking through those very grand hallways, they felt suffocating—a confining, immobile space, dead, unlike the hollows, which always had a life of their own.

There were flicking bulbs of light, as though they held trapped Moonglows, hanging from the high ceilings. Portraits of the King lined the walls and crafted items sat within transparent, sharp-edged encasings. One resembled the shell Aunt Xiangmu had served tea in, though more intricate, detailed, shaped like a pear hanging upside down, painted with various pigments.

Whenever we discovered new plants, creatures, species of emerging trees, we marveled from afar rather than uprooting them and shoving them in glass prisons to display. Such transgressions would cause the natural gods to riot, bringing storms and flooding our hollows. Though I had not experienced the wrath of the gods myself, the stories told by Grandmother and other elders in Feng were more than enough to ensure we continued traditions.

When the guards left me in my spacious chamber, I wandered over to the bed, one of the few Land Wanderer furnishings Grandmother had described and prepared me to encounter. Aunt Xiangmu, too, told me I'd be expected to eat, that the Palace would offer me 'Feng foods' though there was no such thing back home. I thought of the tea Aunt Xiangmu had made a show of drinking at her meeting with Copper.

My toes tried to grip at the bone floor, struggling with the polished surface so unlike soil. The bed had clean, unwrinkled sheets embroidered in royal gold patterns matching the golden bed frame and pillars stretching towards the ceiling. A small bone table sat next to the bed with a lamp. I flinched at the sight. I missed the woodchips. Everything here was too lifeless.

I'd been informed I would not meet with the King until the wedding, as per their customs. It was strange to keep the soon-to-be married couple apart, without intimacy, connection—love. But of course they didn't care. To think my sisters had such glorified imaginations of this place and its people.

There was a knock, and I hurried to the door.

When I opened it, a short Land Wanderer stood with

a raised hand, as if surprised by my appearance. I stepped aside to allow her entrance. She took quick, delicate steps inside, as though guided by the wind, and closed the door behind her. Similar to the guards, her hood covered all but her lips.

"Lady Liu." She bowed. "You need not rise to welcome me but simply call your permission for me to enter."

In Feng, we rushed to greet those who visited our hollows upon seeing them by open entrances. We welcomed all visitors as family. It seemed like a rude custom not to physically greet someone by the door.

From within the Land Wanderer's beige cloak, she pulled out a pair of woven white silk shoes.

I took a step back, feeling the smooth bone walls behind me, then flinched away from them. "No, thank you." I raised a hand and pulled my brown travel-cloak tighter around me.

"Please, I will be reprimanded, punished, if—if you do not take them…" The young being's voice sounded far too young and afraid, but her words held a hint of a threat.

The Land Walker explained she was a Tasker. We had no such thing in Feng. We didn't have specific roles, or rather our roles were ever-changing—though for the Elder and her family, our family, to lead, to protect was our primary duty. The thought of the Palace's idea of roles and order as an indication of superiority and inferiority left a bitter taste.

I hesitated before approaching her to take the shoes. "What is your name?" I attempted to catch a glimpse of her face.

The Tasker bowed lower. "It is unimportant. You may refer to me as the Tasker." I was disheartened by her response, but neither she nor I were here to make friends, even though the thought disheartened me.

Without another word, she left before I could ask about my mother and sisters.

I drifted towards the window, tossing the slippers aside as soon as the door shut. I hauled open the metal screen with my eyes closed, the sound a blood-curdling cry. The white cloths on the windows stood in stark contrast to my brown cloak. In the distance, the healers, adorned in green, were preparing the land for regrowth. The younglings weaved between those who towered above them. In their hands sat small pouches of seeds.

One older healer, after bringing a young oak tree to its infancy, fell onto her knees. Her cloak shed from her back, fluttering onto the ground. The roots of her needle threads greyed, spreading like frost over red maple. The other healers gathered. They were finished for the day, but they knew a member would leave them. I leaned out the window, wishing to join them, until they disappeared along with the setting sun.

The small lamp next to my bedside was not filled with fire or Moonglows. It contained lightning, waiting to burst from the glass, seeking to destroy. My fingers floated over the small protrusion on the lamp's base. The light flickered and drained from the room, leaving me with only an uncomfortable, static hum and pale moonlight.

When my lids fell slack, rather than restful slumber, I lay stiff on the cold floor, fingers carving, slowly, into the wall under the window, hidden behind the cloth, images of storm trees, Memory Clouds, and what I remembered of my mother's features, before drawing Chuiliu's eyes—wide and doe-like as I drifted to sleep.

In my dream, a map unfurled. I knew it held the way around the Palace, and a plan to take the King's life. Yet, the map remained blank no matter how hard I stared at the aged parchment.

My mind reacted like a trapped animal, panicked, desperate. I would've never had such thoughts before— to plot, to kill. If my sisters could see me now...

Would Grandmother be disappointed?

In the middle of the night, I found myself too restless for sleep. I tugged a metal keeper used to store different items over my carvings. I didn't want to expose my homesickness in case it was to be used against me, though I'd often been told by Grandmother I wore my emotions like needle threads on my head.

I crept towards my door, opening it with a gentle

creak. Much to my surprise, there was no one outside. Suspicion tingled at the bottoms of my feet. It was far too noiseless for the number of people I'd seen traveling into and out of the Palace from Feng. Perhaps many were asleep in bed, but surely there would still be sounds.

The paintings of Land Wanderers lining the corridor followed my quiet steps with their seemingly moving irises, chilling me further than the already frigid bone tiles beneath my feet. I avoided their stares as I neared each white, featureless door, unable to tell how it might be possible to access what was within.

Many of the hallways seemed as though they should extend farther but didn't. Windows sat in intervals with cloths pooling from the top. Outside, Feng stretched wide and endless. Where the Palace melted into the long stretch of wall, as though encased in a mold.

I passed a dozen doors and corridor openings before reaching the end of the hall. Around the corner, there was a new corridor that came to an abrupt halt at a wall. Muffled murmurs seeped through.

I rushed to the wall, hoping no one would be in the rooms I passed, but also hoping someone would be. It would make the Palace feel less empty. I pressed my ear against the bone, the cold shocking the warmth of my bark, my body resisting every second of the contact. I heard the shuffling of feet.

No door was in sight, so I searched the walls for

an opening. There was a slight drift along the ground where the wall wasn't sealed. On all fours, I neared the opening, hoping to catch conversation. As though carried by the wind, whispers came like faint whistles.

"Is the procedure almost complete?" A low voice.

"Yes, and if successful..." a mellow voice trailed off. "Those poor people."

"Think about yourself first. And your family." This one was barely audible.

"Why are you awake, Lady Liu?"

I scrambled onto my feet with a yelp to see my Tasker at the corner. She peeked at me with a nervous stare.

Above her, nestled where the wall and ceiling met at the corner of the hallway, was a dark orb. Many of the same were present throughout the Palace. Like a watching eye, a pupil without the white. There was something similar back in Feng, though I'd originally thought it was a bird, always perched high within the tallest trees. Perhaps it had been watching us the whole time.

"I had trouble sleeping." Then I rested a hand against the wall. "What's on the other side?"

"Only certain individuals have access," the Tasker said, hesitant, and seemed in a hurry to guide me away from the wall.

As she led me back to my room, I turned and saw the brief shift of a shadow beneath the slitted opening, and the sound of footsteps stopped.

4

THE MARKET

A phase later, before the sun rose, there was a knock on my door. I sat up before the echo of the first rap had faded and rushed myself onto the bed, pulling on the itchy nightgown the Tasker had given me last night and the uncomfortable white slippers. After my bark's initial rebellion, my mind recognized the softness and comfort, though foreign—something both shocking and welcoming.

"Come in." I lay on the bed with my feet dangling off the edge, swinging side to side. Mother would've chastised me in her soft voice to greet guests properly. Even in her most angry moments, she was calm, only with a slight dent in between her eyes that disappeared as soon as it arrived.

"I have been asked to accompany you to the nearby markets today," the Tasker said when she entered.

"The markets?"

Markets were things I'd only heard of from Grandmother but had never seen myself. Sometimes our gatherers met with the Palace's merchants, offering goods the Palace didn't have, though we only offered what had fallen from bushes, trees, and roots, never uprooting them ourselves.

"For a dress."

I wrinkled my nose, my attention flitting to the nightgown and shoes. Then I stood, pulling on my cloak.

"Lady Liu, your *attire*—" She gestured to what she'd described as the keeper before she noticed I'd moved it and paused. "There are other articles of clothing you can choose from. Ones *appropriate* for outerwear."

I waved a hand, drawing my cloak close around the nightgown, and smiled. "See, you can't even tell."

The Tasker grimaced, then nodded with reluctance when it was clear I wouldn't be giving in. As she led me out of my room, she snuck occasional sideways glances, flinching when she saw the nightgown peeking through.

On each side of the opened front gates perched two guards on Travelers. In the middle was a Traveler at a similar height to Copper's, perhaps even taller. I walked up to the machine, placed a hand against its long bird legs. The cold metal froze my fingertips. The legs creaked, bent, and the half-egg body—looking like a carcass scooped clean of its organs—lowered itself, folding its legs at unnatural angles. Its clawed feet scraped against bone. I shuddered at the sound.

I stepped back. "I would prefer to go by foot."

"Oh no, Lady Liu. It would take far too long."

The Tasker noticed my gaze trained on the Traveler's legs.

"There are different speeds. You'll see."

"I'd much prefer—"

The Tasker lowered her voice. "We are being watched."

I pinched the fabric of my cloak from the inside. It would be much more beneficial to be in the King's good graces so I could approach him, find his weaknesses, question him about my sisters and mother. If I were to at least give the appearance of trying to assimilate to the Palace's ways, perhaps I could earn the King's trust. I whispered an apology to what little wind I was able to borrow since arriving at the suffocating Palace, and felt it leave my feet, my limbs suddenly weighted. I wondered how Land Wanderers endured their entire lives.

"Fine."

My movement was awkward, my limbs jerking as I tried to climb into the Traveler. My knees rammed into its side, pain shooting up my nerves.

My feet met the soft hay-like interior of the machine, and I withdrew into myself when I realized what I was stepping on: creature fur—I jerked back, falling on to the seat with my feet raised before I noticed the seat was made from creature skin. Though my cloak acted as a divide, I imagined the dead beneath me. I strove to keep as little of my body from touching the seat as possible, a balancing act that drew a disapproving glare from the Tasker even though she remained silent. My fingers twitched towards the handle but paused when the material met my eyes—bone, just like everything else in this cursed place.

The Tasker looked up at me from below. "I know this isn't ideal."

All I wanted to do was rip the death from the Traveler and return it all to the earth. It seemed no parts of the creature had been left unused in furnishing this repulsive vehicle.

"Do you see the buttons marked with symbols on the panel in front of you?"

I took a small, shuddering breath, then refocused on the Tasker's words. Small circles sat against a flat surface, each marked with a different drawing in ink. The symbols we used in Feng resembled what it was meant to depict almost to its exact likeness. These were unknown to me.

My eyes darted towards the bone mechanism as the Tasker demonstrated each control, pressing the indented 'buttons.'

"The legs lower and elevate the Traveler. These arrows increase and decrease the speed. The cross halts the machine. There's a controller on the side for shifting directions. For today, I'll maneuver the Traveler for you so you can simply enjoy the journey."

I missed the wind's comforting caress so much it pained me.

The Tasker noticed my distress and gestured to the side of the Traveler. "You can hold the handles if you feel you're about to fall."

I felt myself shrivel internally as I glanced again at the handles. I would rather fall. My hands balled the fabric of my cloak against my lap along with the nightgown within, almost pinching the bark beneath.

The Tasker swung herself onto a Traveler shorter than both mine and the guards'. In the Tasker's hand was a small square bearing the same symbols as those in front of me. She pressed the speed increase arrow. The clink and scrape of the Traveler's feet against the tiles caused my skin to ripple. With a jerk, the machine picked up its pace, and I was flung back against the animal skin; the wind pushing against me was unwilling. My hand flew towards the handles unconsciously. I choked back bile as my fingers curled around the bone, bark filing against the surface.

On the way to the markets, the grass thinned under our Travelers, turning to sand. Unlike the humidity and dampness of Feng, the air here was thin and choking, dizzying my head. I sucked drying breaths through my nose, the sand particles scratching my nostrils and throat, and I struggled to keep my eyes open. The Tasker yelled for me to keep my head down, pulling my cloak over my face, and apologized over and over for forgetting to give me a 'Straining Mask.'

When we finally stopped, I stumbled off the Traveler, my throat no longer willing to constrict and hold down the sickness, the suckers waiting to erupt. Sap streamed down my face, my eyes exhausted from trying to expel the sand. I'd not yet learned how to borrow the wind with my hands, only my feet.

"It gets easier." The Tasker offered a meek smile.

I glared with my half-squinting eyes still burning, bile dripping from my mouth held agape. Though I admit the Traveler was indeed fast, I couldn't imagine anyone wanting to be tossed from side to side in this contraption.

"Have you ever travelled to the Glace in the west and the Clay in the east, Lady Liu?" the Tasker asked.

I rested one hand on my Traveler, still bent over and straining to stay upright, loathing every second of the contact. My nose seared when I tried to breathe again. Whether or not it became easier, it would be a long while before I'd get on another one of these horrible machines.

"I've heard only stories, tales from my grandmother," I gasped, trying to calm my shuddering breaths. "I've never left the south, left Feng, before."

The Tasker frowned, though I wasn't sure if it was

for my lack of knowledge about the world outside Feng or for my suffering—perhaps both.

"We trade with the people there, and many of their merchants travel to our markets as well. What you see—"

"Do the tiles stretch as far as Glace and Clay?" I asked.

"Glace and Clay have their own palaces with specific markets in the west and east that we may visit. This is the only one at which all three trade."

I wiped my lips and nose with the back of my hand.

The Tasker hurried to hand me a handkerchief made from a fine material.

"Silk," she offered.

I marveled at the purposeful stitching of the Palace on its surface, the King's face on the reverse; crowning his head were silver locks which poured over his shoulders, ending just below, the rest of the body unsewn.

"Lady Liu, please return to your Traveler. We have no time to waste!"

I grimaced at the dreaded contraption a century-aged trunk's length away.

"If we finish early, do we have to hurry back right away?" I asked, still queasy.

"We can sit for a moment if we finish early," she said with a small smile.

"Alright," I said. "Can I walk instead?"

The Tasker hesitated before also getting off her Traveler.

"Oh, there's no need—"

She shook her head vigorously. "I would be expelled from the Palace! If you so choose to walk on foot—I, too, will do the same."

I appreciated her dedication to her duties, but I wished she wouldn't be so docile. I supposed I shouldn't criticize, given my obedience to Grandmother.

The guards remained on their Travelers, and I tried not to gawk as the Tasker maneuvered ours to follow. Without occupants, they resembled headless birds missing half their bodies.

As we neared the market, I spotted the rows of shops and stalls. Some were staggered in their positioning, though most were in a uniform line with the designs differing based on where the merchant was from. Wafting towards us were scents reminiscent of Feng, mixed with the metallic tang of the Palace, and others wholly unfamiliar—those must be from Glace and the Clay: an inviting earthy scent mixed with cooled flames and flowing waterfalls.

Some stallholders sat behind small structures erected with carved planks of wood and clay, others perched on clay stools under dried mud-tiled roofs, some stood in front of open huts constructed from hay and wild grass or dead pieces of wood from storm trees. The merchants from the Palace were easiest to spot. Their stalls and shops had white tiles lined over the dirt floor and large metal slabs overhanging as roofs.

As we moved through the market, nearest to us was a merchant with fruits—deep purple-red—laid out. With a thin blade, they sliced them in half, peeled back the skin, and placed the naked flesh on a large, saturated dried leaf. A muscled arm appeared from underneath their sand-colored cloak and beckoned in our direction.

"Lady Liu, we—"

I raised a hand.

"Cactus pear," they said, "straight from the deserts of Clay."

I removed the fruit from the leaf and brought it close to me. It smelled like the rich honey of bee hives occasionally found nestled in storm trees, though lighter. And though we didn't eat in Feng, I found the fruit enticing. If I'd be forced later to consume, I'd rather the first be a choice I made myself.

I closed my eyes, hesitant, as I took my first bite. It was as sweet as its scent but with a slight tang, and the sensation of the fruit's flesh moving down my throat felt like damp moss. Before I could take another bite, the Tasker reclaimed my attention with a voice more urgent than before.

"The dress first, then we can visit the other merchants and artisans while we wait for the Designer to work." The way they said *Designer* made it seem as though this being was of upmost importance.

The Tasker approached the merchant and handed them a copper coin. In Feng, there was trading and exchanges among us, though it was more so an exchange of knowledge and of stories. We requested nothing in return for offering a helping hand. To think so many like the chief had left their old life behind, I couldn't understand. Maybe what appealed to them was the wonder, the curiosity, that my sisters had often spoken about. I wondered if any of those who had left their homes ever regretted their decision.

It was strange. This market. The merchants. But the rowdy yet peaceful atmosphere reminded me of when those in Feng would gather, enjoy the passing breezes in quiet while the younglings hid and chased one another in a game of Seekers.

I had thought the King simply wanted to erect palaces across all the lands and pave over the natural world until there was nothing left and no one to go against his desires. These markets refuted some of my previous assumptions about the King; I refused to believe his intentions were good. Yet, these beings here seemed content rather than made up of broken families and torn-apart homes, the way the King had been condemning us and ours.

The Tasker took me through the market, gesturing to the small pendants, vases, plates and masks made from clay and glass. I ran a finger over the smooth surface of a transparent vase with a black-inked tree, a species unknown to me—one barren with only branches, unlike the storm trees—at a Glace artisan shop. Sap rushed to my cheeks when I realized I'd left a minor scratch and the Tasker had to trade for it. The artisan's shoulder tensed as they polished the silver coin the Tasker handed them against their royal-blue cloak.

It was all so unnecessary—to create these objects, to wear them, to display them. Yet there was a strange allure about it all—the same way I found myself drawn to collecting different withered plants and fallen flowers.

"You're free to choose the fabric and colors of your dress, and the accessories can be from any merchant. Though, you must choose an item each from Glace, Clay, the Palace, and Feng. Each artisan has their specific mark. You'll notice it on the pieces you choose to purchase."

I scoured the vase for any signs of a mark. The Tasker noticed my curiosity and raised the glass, revealing the flat bottom. There was small ink tree within a circle.

I tapped the mark. "Can you not easily copy it?"

The Tasker smiled, more animated and friendly than before. "Perhaps. I have seen it done. But the trader must live with the fact that the art is not their own. Though there are certainly some who don't care—" She raised a gold coin, waved it, before returning it to the pouch at her hip, beneath her beige cloak. "Now, shall we?"

The Tasker was much more relaxed here than at the Palace, perhaps because of the uplifting atmosphere, or because Copper and the King were not present. Regardless, I much preferred her like this. Likely she'd return to that same subdued state upon return. For now, she felt almost like a friend, and I wondered if she might finally tell me her name. Before I could ask, the Tasker had already moved along.

Near the center of the market stood a Land Walker by the entrance of his shop, speaking with another merchant. His sweep of dark hair rose at the front and cascaded into a warm beige halfway down his back, distinct compared to the others of his kind with short, cropped hair hanging above their shoulders or cut close to their heads.

"Designer," the Tasker said as we approached.

A welcoming expression graced his drawn features.

"Call me Z." The Designer offered a palm and a bow. "Short for Zinc." He winked, which emphasized his gold-lined lashes, framing green eyes. I wondered if perhaps he'd gotten sand in his eye the way I had.

I placed my hand in his, marveling at his blue-painted lips with orange-lined edges. When he raised his head, I caught a hint of the tattoos that stretched along his neck and collarbone: I realized with a jolt that they were the same images as the ones carved into the Palace's doorway.

"Your dress is"—humor creasing the edges of his eyes—"quite striking."

The Tasker looked at me as if to say she knew someone would notice, but I avoided her glare and redirected Zinc's attention. I pulled my hand back, and my fingers drifted to the cloak he wore, made from a material resembling what storm worms spun. The texture's resemblance to my own cloak was uncanny, but the weave was different. Rather than unpredictable zigzags, it was in uniform crosses.

"The weaving is so symmetrical. How was this made? Is it storm-worm silk?" I asked.

He looked down, his striking eyes softening with admiration.

"We grow it... elsewhere." His smirk was playful, boastful even—one I hadn't seen in a while. Heshi was always coy, much like Zinc was now. With a grand sweep of the arm and a bashful smile, Zinc said, "Might I interest you in a photograph then?"

Photograph. The word was one unfamiliar to me, and I shifted in anticipation, eager but afraid to see what it was.

He reached in his cloak and brought out a small square, a too realistic drawing. Rows and rows of vines and sprouting buds, triangular spiked leaves, and hanging fruit sat uniform—a stark contrast to what we grew in Feng; untamed, which was what I loved most.

"These fields grow medicinal herbs and some of the more adaptable plants from Feng. We trade for seeds from your gatherers."

We made portraits for the walls of our hollows from what we collected from the ground, hand-painted them onto river rocks using pigment from fruits and inedible plants. I'd never seen such a thing as a photograph, capturing its subject so accurately. Zinc placed it in my hand, angling his body so the Tasker could see the gesture but not what I held. The thickness of it surprised me—until I realized there was more than one. Zinc looked at the Tasker, then looked back. *Shh*.

When I lowered the photograph, Zinc had already made his way to the back of his shop and held aside a curtain made from glass, clay, and bone beads woven together in a hemp braid, waiting.

In the room, there were walls lined with fabric organized into different colorful rolls with smaller pieces of the same materials displayed on tables just beneath. It resembled the main area, but there was a rectangular machine with a base resting at the height of my waist. There was a suspended arm attached, ending in the sharp point of a needle.

"This is the lovely contraption I used to create the cloak, and soon, your dress." Zinc had a dreamlike expression. "The merchants and artisans here are not the most advanced in technology and machinery use, but you'll probably encounter far more magnificent things the farther north you go, over the walls—even more fascinating than the Travelers and Ground Turners. But, I take it, like your mother and sisters, *the King* wants to introduce you slowly, so as not to shock you. And hopefully—" Zinc's words strung together like riddles, as though he was trying to tell me something without directly saying it.

"Designer—" The Tasker's tone was a warning, edged with irritation as she lowered herself into a bow. She glanced quickly behind her.

Zinc's expression faltered, then he flung a sharp look at the Tasker.

"My mother and sisters?" I asked.

"Lady—"

I waved a hand to silence the Tasker.

"They were here?" My eyes locked with Zinc's.

He tilted his head to the side, amused. "Yes. And the most marvelous dresses they had made for them, the finest silks they chose."

"Are they—?"

"Lady Liu."

Zinc scuttled back a few steps. He had a curious grin, attention darting to the photographs still in my hand before clearing his expression entirely and rearranging it to one of coy submission.

I took the signal and slipped the photographs inside my cloak before turning to see Copper by the shop opening, the hood of her white cloak drawn up. A few seconds later, two guards appeared at her side. Already, a small crowd was growing outside of Zinc's shop when Copper lowered her hood.

"Keeper Copper—"

Copper held up a hand to silence the Tasker. "Now, now. There's no need for a big entrance." She smiled, then stared directly at me. "We're all *family* here, aren't we?"

The Tasker bowed, then situated herself next to Zinc.

"You seem to be enjoying yourself, Lady Liu." Copper flashed her teeth. "But we are on *quite* the schedule, and the Designer here is rather busy himself, aren't you?" Her eyes bored into the top of Zinc's bowed head. Zinc didn't rise but flicked his eyes upwards. An eye roll. I was surprised Copper allowed such disrespect.

"Oh yes, *very busy*, I suppose." He nodded, perhaps a bit too vigorously, then turned to me. "Please, Lady Liu. Let me show you our finest silks. You won't be disappointed. And perhaps something to remind you of home." He looked to Copper before returning his attention to me.

"That would be perfect," I said with a genuine smile.

Copper sniffed but remained silent, as if actively trying to hold her tongue.

When I followed Copper out, my hand never left the hidden photographs.

We stopped by a booth not far from the shop. Copper requested two glass bottles of red liquid, handing them to the guards trailing behind her, then requested two glasses to sample. It resembled the blood that ran through Land Wanderer veins.

"Wine," Copper said. "Some of the finest around here. Aged, made from grapes. You have no such thing in Feng, do you?"

We have no need.

Copper explained the wine's intoxicating qualities, sometimes calming. I thought of the relaxing hush of the trickling rivers in Feng—its alluring whispers in the darkest hours of the night, the slight vibration it caused in the grounds of our hollows, its coolness on our bark. I wondered if they were similar—the wine and the rivers.

The smell was heavy, rich fruit mixed with moss. She raised her glass, and held out the other, silently beckoning me to take it. I recoiled, but with the crowd gathered in front of Zinc's shop, I'd no choice but to comply.

A single sip, and I had to hold back a gag.

"Delicious, isn't it? Mind-dizzying and *perfect* for celebrations." Copper winked. The action, I realized, was intentional, not simply dirt finding its way into the eye. On Zinc, it was odd, too forced, but Copper made it seem natural, fluid.

I mustered a grin and handed the Tasker my glass. "I'll save it for later."

Copper regarded me with silent curiosity.

We ended up taking the Traveler back because Copper made it clear I had no choice in this either. I managed not to throw up, thankful I kept down the food the Tasker introduced to me: an oil-fried peanut powder delicacy purchased from another Clay merchant. The Tasker described the tastes as sugary and salty. Somehow, it filled me much more than the sun's rays, the moon's glow, and the rivers' clear rapids. It was a different satisfaction, I suppose.

I endured the journey back to the Palace and had to rest my aching back and churning stomach by lying down as the sun set. I refused to use the bed, though the ground was far too cold, so I tossed both the pillow and blanket under the window, next to my carvings, imagining them as woodchips. Though I couldn't help but admit they were far more comfortable than woodchips.

Before I drifted, I remembered the photographs and rose to fetch my cloak.

On my table, just under the lamp, now sat four neatly placed accessories—chosen under the scrutinizing gaze of Copper: Glace glass earrings in the shape of tears, a swirl of a Clay pendant fired in the kilns—along with a basket of goods. I forwent the chain in favor of the jade necklace still around my collar. From the Palace merchant, I had no choice in the bone bangle with sapphire accents—they sold nothing without bone. And an anklet from Feng, of crawling vines that extended up to my knee.

I returned to my bed on the ground with my cloak and the photographs in hand, sliding out the other squares stacked behind the one of fields. Air halted before reaching my lungs when I saw the first photograph. It was unclear, a grainy black and white, but I could make out my mother sitting with her hands loose on her lap, a gentle grin on her face. She wore a Palace dress with her Feng cloak draped over her shoulders. I lingered on every detail, taking in each line that had appeared on her face. She looked weary yet somehow still content— Mother always saw the positive side in even the bleakest of situations. It ached me to see her strength and the pain lingering beneath her smile.

It took me a long time to move onto the next photograph. I wished to see her again.

The second was still black and white, but with greater clarity. It was my sister... Yunshu. She held a similar pose to Mother, with hands folded on her lap, slightly turned to the side. Her chin tilted upwards and dangling below were several necklaces with chains, both thin and thick, and pendants of varying sizes and designs. Bangles lined up along one puffy-sleeved arm. In her hair were large feathers circling a braided bun. As a youngling, she'd always pick flowers, even though it was forbidden, and weave them into her needle threads. But I would snatch them from her braids when Grandmother neared.

The third photograph was in color, though not painted. I wasn't sure how it was possible. Like Yunshu, Heshi was adorned in elaborate jewelry, a glittering dress resembling the scales of fish, eyes drawn like forest cats, and lips a red crescent moon. Her smile and teeth resembled Copper's. It was only a photograph, yet Heshi's face looked too smooth, like her skin had been sanded down along with her limbs, and the dress she wore exposed half of each arm and leg. Her hair was too fine, like silk, rather than the unruly thick needle threads that once tumbled freely. This looked exactly like something, *someone* she wanted to become.

The fourth photograph held images of someone I knew not, someone with barked skin unsmooth, dark needle threads hanging from their limbs were woven. Perhaps a mistaken inclusion.

The last photograph was a small glass square that only held Sangshu's ghost-like appearance. She was older, more worn, and she still had on her Feng cloak, along with her rough bark skin and needle threads. The image began to move, and I almost dropped the glass. Sangshu's face rotated in a slow circle. Above it floated thin symbols I couldn't read. At the end of the strange scrawl sat a skull. That could mean nothing good.

For a second, Sangshu's face wavered. She blinked, then her lips moved. That was when I dropped the glass onto the bed, staring with a hand raised over my mouth.

"—sister." Sangshu's familiar voice sounded almost strange coming from the photograph, mixed with a slight crackle. The full message seemed to be cut. Nonetheless, her words shook me. "You are the oldest, but you were never our guide—you were always the guided—"

This was the first time she had ever voiced such thoughts. As a child, she was even quieter than Chuiliu. The sap within me ran quicker, heat racing up my limbs. My mind went through a dozen explanations for her words, but there was nothing hidden to search for. The straightforward tone, smooth expression, was what unsettled me most. I had tried my best to put my younger sisters first, to protect them. Yet, I knew I was not enough. They always rebelled against me, as they had rebelled against Grandmother. Nothing about our home made them truly happy.

The sudden rush of memories attacked me as I recalled Yunshu and Heshi's shared whispers as they perched on storm trees, giggling at their wishes and dreams unrelated to their home and much less the duties of which I bared the brunt; of their rebellion when Grandmother told me to fetch them, their ringing laughter bouncing as they flitted away. When they finally returned, Grandmother always looked at me with disappointment. And in the distance, Sangshu was always silent and always watching.

Chuiliu was far too loving and accepting to pass cruel judgements like my other sisters, and I suppose that was why we shared the closest bond.

With simmering anger, I swiped at the glass, now devoid of Sangshu's image, and flung it across the room with such force the photograph cracked down the middle, Sangshu's statement still echoing in my ears. As much as I missed her, her words left a lingering wound.

A wail, not a sound I had ever made before, left me. Even knowing my sisters might've loathed me, I couldn't help but understand. As much as they whispered behind me, I wished for their return. But if it wasn't what they wanted, would it be selfish to convince them to come home? I wondered if Chuiliu might one moon choose the Palace—I'd only hope it would be a choice she herself made, rather than one forced.

5

THE PORTRAITS

There were only seven moons until the ceremony, but the wait was far too long with the knowledge of the photographs—and I willed them to be a confirmation that Mother and my sisters were still alive. Remaining idle in my room would only serve to increase my anxiety. Perhaps they were within this Palace; perhaps we could figure out a plan to escape together—or at least with Mother and Sangshu if Heshi and Yunshu refused to leave.

When I crept out of my room, I found it strange that the halls were empty of all guards, unlike when I first arrived at the Palace. I maneuvered myself with quiet steps past where I'd already explored, heading in the opposite direction and rounding the corner that took me down a new hall. Halfway through, I spotted a strange painting, different from the Land Wanderer portraits. It was a map of sorts. Clusters of trees sat spread out at the bottom. Across the middle, the smile of a moon cut through, containing the trees, the water, the desert within its arc. Marked along the arc were tiny triangles, three of them. The left side was filled with what resembled water, waves, in dark blue. One of the triangles peeked from behind—Glace perhaps. On the right were dunes just below. Clay, surely. The other side of the wall was blank, left unpainted. But I knew there had to be something else.

I searched the map for the market and noticed a small smattering in front of the palace at the center. I left the map behind, not wanting to linger for too long.

Unlike the other hallway wings, this one didn't have tens of rooms, only seven, yet somehow stretched further than the rest. It was also the only one with a slight breeze. On the door nearest the hallway opening was a square of smoothed-out bone, and engraved upon it was a portrait of my face with uncanny likeness.

I winced, withdrawing into myself, wondering if I was to move into this room after the ceremony.

To my surprise, the other doors had portraits as well: of my mother and sisters. Mother's was right by a door looming at twice the height of the others, almost brushing the ceiling. On it sat an engraved portrait that had been shaved off, leaving faint outlines that made it impossible to discern who it was.

There was one more door near the entrance of the

hall, blank, and I couldn't help but think of Chuiliu. I was hopeful that perhaps Mother and my sisters were indeed behind these doors, but the thought also filled me with dread—how suffocating it must be to be enclosed within these walls.

Just as I was about to knock on the door with Sangshu's portrait, at the end of the hall, the largest door swung outwards as if pushed over by a gust of wind. Filling the frame was the King, still in his bone-white cloak, face hidden beneath the hood so much so even his chin couldn't be seen. The only indication that suggested it was him was when his voice echoed, carried down the hall towards me as though arriving on a rogue drift:

"What are you doing here?"

My thoughts were not sorted enough for anything coherent. "My family—"

He laughed—the sound tortured, dark, like the rumble of an earthquake, and as it faded out into dense echoes, though it was slight, it held a quiver. Then, it looked as though he wanted to reach out towards me as he raised his hand, swallowed within his cloak. He dropped it in an instant, as though afraid, when a weight landed on my shoulder.

But no one was there when I turned. I looked back to the King's door; it sat shut, as though it'd never been opened.

6

THE ROOM

With the King gone, I tapped all the other doors in the hall, quietly, and received no response. I couldn't tell if I was relieved or disappointed as I lingered in front of the room with Mother's portrait before leaving the hall.

At the mouth of the corridor, I noticed the dark orbs nestled in the corners of the ceiling. It felt as though someone was always watching, even though I was allowed to roam freely. *Too freely*, as though that was what they wanted me to do.

I passed the halls I'd explored previously, avoiding the creeping portraits' eyes. Still no one came into sight. Around a corner, several corridors past the one with the rooms holding my family's portraits, there was a door at a dead end. It was made of dull iron, rather than bone like the others, with a strange symbol engraved on its surface.

There was a small sliver of an opening, enough for me to wiggle in a finger or two. Someone had left the room open. It seemed a bit too convenient, but curiosity had me prying at the door, willing it to fully open as I pulled with what little strength my fingers offered. It didn't budge. I turned several times to peek behind me even though there was still no one there. Panic gnawed at the back of my neck, an itch growing, as though the bark there might peel.

Using the slight breeze coming from the inside of the room, I borrowed the wind to help me in my efforts. The familiar tingle tickled my feet and the palms of my hands. This was the first time I had ever directed the wind to my hands. I prayed it would work.

It didn't. So, I tried again and again, recalling the fading feeling of the wind, drawing it to my feet, bringing it up to my hands, whispering for forgiveness, whispering a request for strength.

The door shifted. I had a chilling feeling it wasn't by my efforts.

My shuddering sigh mingled with the stronger current of cold air from the room. I slipped quickly through the gap. It would be impossible to close the door and open it again to escape if anyone were to come down this way, if someone were to shut the door while I was still inside... My mind conjured the worst possibility upon discovery: the wrath of the King, being expelled from the Palace and dishonoring

Grandmother, dishonoring Feng—and the direst consequence of all, Chuiliu replacing me as the King's next bride.

When my eyes adjusted to the darkness, I caught sight of several metal eggs, as tall as budding trees, arranged in a semi-circle. In the middle of each egg was a small oval window revealing its contents. There was nothing in the first or the second, but the third held a face with closed eyes. Their features were a strange rippling mixture of bark, skin, and what seemed to be a stream running beneath thin membrane—like those from Glace I'd seen at the market.

They appeared to be a young child. One who reminded me of Chuiliu. But I was roused from my thoughts when a low, gurgling cry escaped from their mouth.

They must be in pain.

Without a second thought, I rushed towards the metal egg, thinking of my sisters, squinting at its body to find an opening. At one side, there was a large metal latch. As I heaved, the gurgling mixed with the sound of choking. Bubbles escaped the lips of the being within the metal chamber.

"I'm trying, I'm trying!" I whispered.

The latch flipped open, and I was flung onto my back as the door knocked into me. Out drained the liquid, a blue-green waterfall, but as it pooled by my feet, I realized its texture was much thicker than water. The being tumbled out, coughing and spluttering. Their knees connected with the bone beneath us with a crack as they landed on all fours.

With hesitance, I crawled closer. "Are you okay—?"

They tossed their head, shoulder-length needle threads flying, and sneered, voice scratchy. "*What* are you doing? *Why* did you do that?"

I flinched at the throaty screech that left the figure. And scampered back. The being was older than I'd first assumed—closer to my age, maybe older. It was hard to tell with the thick liquid still coating most of his naked body. I scrambled to stand.

"I-I thought you needed help. I thought you were stuck I—"

The being barked a laugh. "I don't need help." He looked back at the empty chamber still slick with blue-green ooze.

"Who," I marveled at our resemblance, the curve of his nose that resembled Mother, the thinness of his lips like Yunshu, the slight downwards tilt of his eyes like Chuiliu, "are you?"

A small gust of wind by the man's feet drifted towards me, surrounding me, prodding at my shoes. Suddenly I felt embarrassed, wanting nothing more than to kick off the fabric rubbing against my bark—fabric that I'd come to find comfortable... *natural* even, though the thought made me queasy. Treading on the uneven ground of Feng, sleeping on woodchips and waking with loose earth in my hair wasn't as appealing as when I had first arrived at the Palace, when homesickness had attacked me full force. Now it was only a dull murmur of a past I wanted to hold onto.

The humorous gleam in the being's eye shifted to curiosity. Especially in his nakedness, the being looked more like he was from Feng than I did. "I could ask you the same question."

The being then refocused on the liquid that pooled around us. It had soaked through my nightgown and cloak. With a sweep, he brought up his hand, squinting as he concentrated on the slimy substance. The murky ooze of blue-green moved with his gestures, whisked up by an unseen force and began pooling back into the opened shell, hovering within, clinging onto the metal interior—unspilling. A Water Shifter? I thought of their bodies made of liquid, some fresh water, some the salt of seas, that Mother once told me of with a faraway expression—those who could borrow and shift water the way those in Feng could with the wind. From Glace? Impossible with his appearance, surely.

In the ceiling's corner, a familiar dark orb began flashing red, drenching the two of us in its ominous light. I should've known. I'd crossed a boundary the King didn't wish for me to cross.

In a panic, I fumbled my way out of the room, leaving the door open, not wanting to risk being discovered. But when it closed behind me, I knew it must have been the being's work. Though he'd been slumbering, and I thought him disorientated, he was far more alert than I had expected. I rushed back to my room, but the wind left me as soon as I fled, slowing my steps. Guards materialized from around the corner and thundered down the hall towards me. I dove behind the long heavy cloths hanging by the window just as they marched past. I held a hand over my mouth, my panicked breath burning against rough bark.

I waited for the quiet to return before moving once more, but I kept to the walls and halted, skittish at the slightest of noises. I was steps away from my room when Copper appeared, so I ducked to the side behind the opaque foundation of a display case as she whisked past with a troubled expression.

"Lufeng?" she whispered. I dared not respond in case it was a trap, an attempt to get me to reveal myself and my transgression.

When she disappeared down the hall, I snuck back into my room. Without a second thought, I flung myself into the floor nest, the blue-green liquid soaking the white blanket and pillows. My thoughts were too wrapped around the strange being to care. I tossed my soiled shoes near the window to dry.

A knock. Black dots swirled in front of me, blotting out the room.

"One moment!" I rushed to pull on new clothes from the keeper—a putrid yellow dress. I pushed both my nightgown and cloak under my bed, flinching at the dampness.

Just as I was about to allow the Tasker to enter, I noticed the photographs still scattered on the bed. I scrambled to hide them and pick up the fractured glass with Sangshu's message, before sliding everything under the bed.

"Yes, come in," I said, breathless.

She seemed surprised at the dress I was wearing, willingly. The Tasker seemed to forget why she had come for a moment as she looked around the room, making me keenly aware of everything currently hidden under my bed, before she snapped out of her thoughts. "Oh yes, it's time for dinner. Would you like to have it in the dining hall today?"

"Will the King be there?" I asked.

"Yes. He will be present."

Even though I was in no state to ambush him, much less kill him, perhaps I could scrutinize his weaknesses, draw from him answers. I was surprised he would go against his own customs to meet before the wedding when he seemed so firm on other rules.

"Then I shall join him." But my mind continued to linger on the being in the chamber.

7

THE HALL

"The wedding ceremony will also take place in the dining hall," the Tasker said as we made our way towards it.

My feet shuffled bare because I'd forgotten the shoes in my haste. They felt oddly naked without them. It had become an unknowingly familiar feeling to have fabric against my bark, comforting even, compared to the cold bone pressing against my soles. The lesser of two evils. Part of me shook at the growing reliance I had developed for the shoes and feared that the soil in Feng would no longer feel as comforting, if there was even a possibility of return.

Halfway down the hall, the Tasker finally realized my shoeless state. Rather than questioning where they'd gone, she left me with the guards to fetch another pair, rushing back out of nowhere only a few moments later and passing them to me.

I winced at how keenly I slipped them on.

"The other Taskers have been informed of Feng traditions. If there have been any changes over the years—"

"No, nothing has changed." Grandmother was never one to fix what wasn't broken. Even though people left Feng, those who remained were content with their lives. The thought of the delicacies from the market came to my mind. It saddened me for a moment that there would be none in Feng. I quickly banished the treacherous thought.

I wondered if Grandmother would be present at the wedding. Never had she attended one of these ceremonies—except for Mother's, when she had also brought Aunt Xiangmu and some of our close relatives. And as though reading my mind, the Tasker said, "I believe your Elder will be present at the wedding this time."

I paused. It unsettled me to think Grandmother would soon step from the safety of Feng, but it also comforted me knowing I'd see a familiar face.

Doors opened to a dimly lit, grand dining hall. Long rectangular tables with white cloths were lined up perpendicular to each corner, creating the shape of an empty diamond. I stood at its base by the entrance. There was no one else in the hall but us and the King and his Tasker.

I looked around to get a sense of the space. There must be a way for me to gain advantage, secure a weapon unnoticed either prior to the wedding or during. Though the latter would be a greater risk.

The Tasker gestured towards the King, signaling I would walk across the hall alone. He sat at the tip of the diamond at a single round table with a wired lantern in the middle—a small glass eye turned to its side emitting a false glow, an unnatural flame. The King's arms rested at each side of the lantern. He hid his face beneath his white hood, but the light illuminated his lips, pale, bloodless.

Behind the King was a wall made up entirely of stained glass.

Though I tried to move quietly, my steps were thunderous, and with each tread, my hatred for the King grew. I refocused elsewhere to calm the contractions spreading through my body. They would no doubt find their way onto my face, and I couldn't risk the King noticing.

Above, there was silver bent into swooping curves like crescents with crystals dangling off the ends, extending in a spiral around the domed ceiling. They glowed with the same false light as the lantern, but much dimmer, as though it might wane at any moment. As beautiful as they were, these crescents paled in comparison to the ever-changing phases of the moon that lit our nights in Feng.

"Come. Sit." The King's booming voice rumbled through me. "I'm glad you found something you liked."

He gestured to my dress, and I felt the urge to rip the yellow fabric off.

When he lifted his face, he didn't seem so ageless; he appeared a decade older than me though he was just as pale, almost blending in with the bone floors. I wondered, after seeing the photographs of my sisters, if he too had been from elsewhere before the Palace. If so, the transformation couldn't have been a painless one. I didn't want to imagine the procedures necessary for the metamorphosis.

"Is it too dark?" His voice travelled towards me. His eyes seemed warmer, softer, with that same hint of vulnerability from when we first met.

It was only when the brief expression disappeared, replaced with a slightly smug smile, that I realized this was not to be considerate of me but to boast of his *technology*. He motioned to a Tasker, whom I hadn't noticed standing next to him when I stopped in front of the table. The lights above brightened, piercing my eyes.

"Wonderful, isn't it? A light we can control, unlike the moon and the sun." The King threw his arms up, the sleeves of his cloak rising, exposing his human flesh. Yet his limbs were not bare but inked—much like Zinc's.

"Have you ever slept under the moon?" I asked.

The King chuckled. "I have. Then I discovered *these* from a travelling merchant." The King gestured above us, then smiled down at the empty plate his Tasker set in front of him. "You may shun them now, but give it some time, you might find yourself thinking differently."

For a moment, I wondered if he might be from Feng, given his answer.

"Like my mother? My sisters?" I didn't want my voice to quiver, but the words leapt from me in a flurry. Grandmother always said I allowed my emotions to control me far too often. Mother was always the rational one. I was never born to lead.

The King's hands curled into fists, clenched tight for a moment, then quickly unfurled, but he left my question unanswered. The Tasker next to him offered a glass of red liquid. *Wine.* He waved a hand, a relaxed gesture, to beckon the Tasker to set the glass down and fill it.

Next to the empty porcelain plates, the silverware looked odd. They resembled not the ones Grandmother had described. My Tasker had offered me 'Feng food' for all my previous meals—I wasn't excited to find out what the King consumed. We had tools in Feng as well, but it was much easier to return those back to the ground, compared to these metallic things they called silverware. But the knife next to his hand was enticing. A potential weapon, perhaps. An opportunity. The knife would be present at the ceremony, I was sure of it. There would be creatures cut open, as Grandmother had warned, and I would make sure the King was one of them.

Even though I made sure my expression showed compliance, I held tight to my murderous plot. Perhaps if I killed him at the ceremony, everyone would see he was not invincible. That they didn't have to blindly follow him, leaving their homes, abandoning their families. My brain conjured vivid images of my fingers plunging towards the King's face, peeling back his mask, at the same moment I would drive the serrated knife into his chest—a beating thing I knew humans had, relied on, would not survive without.

The King allowed a small smile as he gestured to the wine, reminding me of Copper at the market. "Would you like a glass, too?"

I almost allowed a scowl to slip. I would be required to drink at the wedding, as per Palace customs, but so would the King, and I hoped that would inhibit him enough that he wouldn't see my attack coming. The crystal chalice held between his two fingertips glistened dark red.

"Yes." Though I would've loved nothing more than to pour the wine over the King's white robes.

For a moment, the King was amused. "How you have grown." His tone was nostalgic and his expression melancholic, both of which confused me. "You look so much like your mother." It only registered a moment later that he spoke in Breath.

Before I could question him after breaking out of my shock, I smelled the food, and I felt as though my roots had been poisoned at the tips. It reminded me of the time I came across an injured rabbit, legs caught by protruding branches in its escape; and when a sickly deer was pounced upon by a forest cat—the sharp metallic scent, its denseness, was not one I would ever forget.

I only had to hold on until the wedding.

"I will take my meal in my room," I bit out before swiftly leaving the hall.

But I didn't allow the Tasker to enter when she knocked on my door.

Though there was only a phase left until the wedding, I spent all sun on the floor, analyzing the photographs, shuffling them, looking at them in order then out of order.

With desperation, I searched for any hints in the pictures that might tell me of my mother and sisters' location since there was no answer when I had knocked on the doors with the portraits. In the background of Heshi's photograph, there was a vase similar to the one I had marred—crafted by the Glace artisan. Yunshu's photograph had a framed picture of sandy plains in the background. Barely noticeable, I spotted the small purple-red fruit: the cactus pear. Clay. Unfortunately, Mother's photograph gave away no hints to where she might be, and Sangshu's had only her face. But it was a start.

The dress Zinc had made for the ceremony was folded and tucked beneath a silk covering at the edge of the Palace bed. Perhaps Zinc could answer my questions, and if not, I would at least be able to confirm my suspicions about the King being from Feng. Next to my door was a braided rope that connected to a bell outside. The Tasker mentioned I could pull it to call her, though I'd never thought to use it until now. I tugged on the rope, and a deep, muffled clang echoed outside—three times. It took almost no time at all before she arrived.

"Come in." It felt strange for the words to roll so smoothly from my lips, even though the commands and Script tones were once awkward and foreign.

"Lady Liu." The Tasker bowed.

"Would it be possible to arrange for Zinc to visit?" I motioned to the dress laid out on the bed, and for a moment, the Tasker seemed to stiffen, her lip twitched— annoyance? "The dress may require an adjustment. I think I've eaten a bit too much these past moons."

A lie, but I hoped she would believe it.

"I'll see if that can be arranged..."

When the Tasker rushed out, I wrung my hands as I waited for her return. But a short while later she re-entered my room with a solemn expression.

Hopeful, I asked anyway, "Well? Will Zinc be coming?"

"I'm afraid the request has been denied."

My stomach quaked, and disappointment drew my eyes closed. There was no time left.

8

THE CEREMONY

O n the morning of the ceremony, the Tasker brought into my room an item and sat me down in front of it.

She explained it was a reflector. I drew close to it, staring at a strange version of myself. Though I'd seen my reflection in the waters of Feng, I'd never seen such a still image of me, unaltered by the distortion of natural waters and the colors it took on from its surroundings.

The Tasker pulled out powders from an animal-skin pouch, clay-like mixtures of varying hues, not unlike what I'd seen on Copper's face; my sisters', too, in the photographs. She met my gaze in the reflector before looking away quickly. Her eyes were gold—or perhaps it was only a trick of the light. She was far more youthful than I'd realized, with skin like unmarked porcelain.

Though it'd been half a cycle, this was the first time I'd seen the Tasker up close and at such length.

The Tasker pressed one of the powdery substances onto my face, but my bark threatened to repel it as the powder flaked and continued flaking. It made me appear spirit-like but with cheeks too rouged by petals from flowers and eyes lined too dark with pigment. She tamed my needle threads into a tight bun resting low—pulling at times, a bit too harshly. The pins which held flowers on my head pricked my scalp, leaving irritated patches. Unlike the flowers on Aunt Xiangmu's skirts, these were already wilting.

I dreaded the ceremony. I'd hoped spending time in the Tasker's prolonged presence might help calm me since she had reminded me of Chuiliu and the moments we'd spent in the fields tucking fallen petals into one another's needle threads. But lately, it seemed as though her attitude towards me had taken a turn, and I wasn't sure why.

When the Tasker finished, I saw someone familiar: Heshi. The photograph. And the longer I stared, unblinking, the stiffer the trichomes on my face stood, erect.

Zinc's dress was a mixture of the elements of the Palace and the traditional patterns and fabrics of Feng I'd seen at the market, though they were non-existent back at home. The dress was comprised of white, earth, and red patches with flowing sleeves, cinched at the waist. On the skirt, there was a single slit from the thigh down, the opening interrupted only by a tangle of roots and vines, a stitched pattern of gold. The design was so purposeful compared to the simplicity of the cloak I'd brought from home.

"I am told to inform you that you can wear the cloak from Feng if you wish."

To wear the cloak, though permitted, would be an act of defiance—or perhaps a desperate grasp at an escaping identity. To leave the cloak would mean allowing myself to be influenced by the King and the Palace. But this way, I could better gain the King's trust. Perhaps that was what he was testing. Yet, none of it mattered because he would perish at my hands at the ceremony, or I would perish at his.

The cloak, though dry now, had large, faint stains from where the liquid had touched it. Unlike the blankets I'd hidden under the bed, the blue-green color did not show. I would pull it out before I left the room and draw strength from its familiar comfort. If I were to fail in the King's assassination, I would wish to die with a piece of Feng on my shoulders.

I stepped into shoes that matched the dress—these were much stiffer than previous ones—with a low platform tilting my heel upwards. Two Taskers brought into the room a body-length reflector. They closed the window, pulling the cloths and keeper aside, before propping it up against the slatted metal. Luckily, they were all too preoccupied with their task to notice my carvings. Or perhaps they didn't care.

"What do you think?"

Zinc truly was a marvelous designer.

"It's beautiful." But this wasn't me.

The Tasker extended the bone bangle towards me. I wanted nothing more than to fling it out the window. It reminded me far too much of the Traveler's handles. Then she hooked the glass earrings onto my ears. I wouldn't allow them to pierce them—it was unfathomable to even consider manipulating my body the same way they did with the metal. Last was the anklet—a filed tooth the size of a thumb hung from it, a new addition I didn't know about—which she secured onto the leg opposite the slit in the material. The hem of my vine-weaved dress fell over my feet, concealing the white tooth.

The Tasker's eyes fell to the jade ring around my neck. "It might be best to take the ring off." A tinge of nervousness caused her voice to waver.

"I will keep it. Thank you."

My resolution disappointed her, but the Tasker abided by my wish and secured the clay pendant to my necklace. The clay clinked against the jade, a dull sound against the hollow between my collarbones.

"There is one last thing." The Tasker reached back in the silver keeper and took out a single gold feather and a matching gold leaf, then weaved them into my bun. I couldn't help but wonder which poor creature the feather had been plucked from, and if the creature had lived, having only a single feather removed, or whether they too had become a part of the pavings, a new palace, an item sold at the markets.

"You look magnificent." I sensed reluctance in her words.

I felt rotten, my wrist burning from the thought of wearing the dead, as I trailed behind the Tasker to the dining hall.

The setup for the ceremony was the same, though there was a small wooden ritual table placed at the center. On its surface sat a little glass bottle filled with black liquid and a slender carved object with a filed point, slightly longer than a blade of grass, like bark whittled and sanded too smooth on one end. On the other end of the table rested a slim sharpened stone—one similar to what Aunt Xiangmu had used during the bridewealth negotiations. Upon closer inspection, perhaps it wasn't a sharpened stone at all but carved bone.

My hand flew to the ring nestled in between my collarbones, clutching at the jade for comfort.

The King hadn't yet arrived.

"Should I be informed of the Palace's customs before the wedding?" I asked.

The Tasker cast her eyes downward. "Each step will be announced during the ceremony... There may be rituals you do not agree with... Your ignorance may make it easier."

A vein pulsed in my neck. "How?"

"The more you think about it, the harder it may be when the time comes. And based on your reaction at the dinner previously—"

I winced at the thought of the King in the dining hall consuming the flesh and charred carcasses of lives from Feng. I tried to shake the image of Mother and my sisters doing the same, the blood dripping from their lips, coloring their teeth crimson.

"Were my mother and sisters informed?"

"Your mother was. Your sisters were not…"

"I want to know," I said.

"My apologies, Lady Liu"—the Tasker shuffled her feet—"but I have not been given permission."

There was nothing stopping me from making a fool of myself at the ceremony and dishonoring Grandmother. The Tasker picked up my concern.

"Do not worry, Lady Liu. Everything will be alright." I clutched onto the Tasker's words and nodded. I hoped she was right, but I knew she wasn't—and with it came the morbid thought laced with the paranoia that she secretly wanted me to fail.

Then I remembered my plan. None of this would matter after this moon.

I sat alone at the King's table, *our* table. I felt myself transpiring even though the dress material was thin.

"There's no need to be nervous." A whisper in Script came from behind, sending jitters up my spine. The King took his seat next to mine, folding his hands in front of him. Below sat his porcelain plate rimmed with carved Palace symbols and the unnatural, repetitive curling of vine patterns. Next to it was a crystal chalice and silverware. Humans seemed to require so many unnecessary things.

The King's looming figure next to me felt more daunting than ever, causing me to shrink from him, digging scars into my palms.

Two guards pulled open the dining-hall doors, revealing Copper in a dark red dress embroidered with gold, her white cloak marked with faint copper patterns swirling down its length and across the hood. Behind her trailed others dressed similarly, some in pants, some cloak-less and in long robes. Once they had all entered, the guards shut the doors.

I wondered if these were indeed the King's actual family, if they'd altered their appearances like the King had and were once from elsewhere, or if they were simply other individuals who held power in the Palace.

With hope, I searched the faces for Mother's, for my sisters', though it proved to be a futile effort.

Copper took the seat on the right of the King. The others followed suit down the table.

Once everyone had settled, the doors opened once more. Grandmother stood, chin tilted upwards, with

Aunt Xiangmu behind her. Uncles and other aunts, along with older cousins trailed further back—in their brown cloaks, bodies bare, they resembled a floating line of trees. They made their way to the table on my left, Grandmother settling down so close to me I could almost feel the calm, confident aura radiating from her body, and the gentle push of the wind. I watched Copper and Aunt Xiangmu exchange a brief look.

Those from Clay and Glace drifted in wearing sand-colored and dark water-blue cloaks respectively, parting like a waterfall meeting a protruding desert stone as they filled the final two tables—the Clay diagonal from Feng; the Glace diagonal from those of the Palace. I hadn't paid too much attention to the people of Glace at the market, more so hypnotized by their glasswork. Up close, their skin was translucent, the liquid running underneath not the deep red of human blood nor the amber of Feng sap but a colorless rush, like a stream or river which moved like wind currents through a tunnel—the same currents that could sometimes be seen by those who were completely one with the wind.

Seconds after everyone was seated, Taskers flitted from behind the King and me, carrying pitchers, filling our chalices with a dark purple liquid. The King remained still, an almost warm, content smile on his lips as his gaze swept across the hall. Then he lowered his hood, and everyone else mimicked him, including me. His silver eyes shone even brighter in the light. Grandmother didn't look at me. Her eyes remained trained on the setup in the middle of the hall.

The first course, I recognized: a brew made from herbs gathered from Feng, medicinal ones mixed with edible fungi. I brought the brew to my lips and blew before taking a long gulp. The warmth of the tea, almost uncomfortably so, reminded me of how Aunt Xiangmu served Copper cold tea as a smite. Perhaps the intention behind this warm tea was the same.

"It's to your liking?" The King's own brew still sat almost to the brim of the half-shell.

I winced at his voice, reluctantly nodding. If I made him think I was docile perhaps he would lower his guard. As if having a silent conversation with himself, the King's expression was amused. I held a smile of my own, though one only present in my mind. I would let him believe everything was going according to his plan, for now.

The Taskers removed the shells, some empty, some still full, and left the room in tense silence. I breathed out a sigh when the quiet was broken by the Taskers' re-entrance, but the air leaving my lips halted when they placed down a serrated knife in the place of our spoon. The glint of the jagged edges gave away what was to come. Though I'd expected the knife, its appearance—the violence it stood for, the creatures it had cut through—still rattled me.

I made a note to hide the knife in my sleeve when no one was paying attention.

The beast would fall.

I recalled the King's meal and thought of the small squirrels back in Feng. Though this feast likely wouldn't contain the tiny creature's meat, we would be served the cooked flesh of others.

For weddings in Feng, Moonglows would gather, surrounding the pair who entered the river together, walking hand in hand until the water reached their chests. They would plunge their heads beneath rushing currents before locking in an embrace, foreheads pressed together, listening to each other's steady breaths until the rhythmic pounding was in sync before they pulled apart. When they broke the surface again, the wind would carry them out of the river, reintroducing them to Feng as one rather than two separate entities—a spiritual binding. I'd only heard about Feng weddings, whimsical stories told by our people in the hush of night, private affairs I'd never witnessed firsthand. One I once wished for.

Again the scent hit me before the sight as the Taskers carried plates to serve those seated farthest from us first. There were severed limbs and different cuts of unknown flesh. I gripped the cutlery hard until Grandmother and Aunt Xiangmu were served before checking their reaction. In front of Grandmother sat a thick neck broken down. Aunt Xiangmu had the flesh sliced into chunks.

Both remained calm, though a few who sat near the end of the Feng table were having difficulty keeping their expressions neutral at the sight of meat piled high, as though it would topple any moment. On the other side of the room, Copper and her people seemed ready to devour their meal. She tapped the table with her ringed fingers. I dreaded what I'd be served, swallowing back the sour sap threatening to escape up my throat and kept my eyes from squeezing shut.

"For you." The King chuckled—though quiet, to me it boomed.

The Taskers placed a plate in front of us both. At the center of each sat the skull of a deer, and I imagined the breaths it once took drifting as steam out of its nose. Its antlers were still intact, gnarly, tangled, sprouting in different upward directions—bones growing out of bones, the corpse of a dying tree. The sockets where the eyes should've been bored into my own, holding me captive, as though the chasm might pluck out my eyes and consume them, using them as replacements for those the creature had lost. Surrounding the naked skull were various cuts in thick slices, decorated with shredded skin. Every piece was still pink, slightly red even, with blood pooling beneath, as if still alive and in pain, or only recently dead.

The King had taken such a beautiful tradition and twisted it, made it something so vile. To ask me to comply, and in front of our Elder, Grandmother, no less— was savagery. It pained me to think about Mother, my sisters, who'd undergone the same ceremony, and how

Grandmother would've watched Mother as she betrayed Feng and our people, even if it meant temporary peace, a transaction, a merger of sorts, though it wasn't so much a merger as it was a devouring of Feng. Glace and Clay were likely delighted they didn't have to offer their own—or perhaps they already had.

The guards, the Taskers, the builders, too, were people the King had stolen from other lands—willing or unwilling.

The King lifted his knife and fork, cut a large bite and made a show of stretching out his tongue, allowing it to curl around the bleeding flesh, chewing, then swallowing. He took a long sip of his wine, all eyes focused on his every movement. When he set down his chalice, I felt the shift of eyes from the King to me.

The tips of my fingers prickled as I picked up the silverware, the cold handles rattling through me. I pierced a piece so small it wouldn't require the use of the knife and lifted it to my mouth, folding my lips over it so it wouldn't touch. My tongue curdled at the strange, sour taste and unfamiliar texture. The juices slid, greasy, down my throat. When I swallowed, the density of the flesh mixed with the unnatural flavors, spices from the markets massaged into the cooked skin, sat like stones at the bottom of my stomach. Each piece moved down my throat with a loathsome thickness, leaving a grotesque aftertaste, bits of flesh caught on their way down. Sour and salted bile lingered in my mouth, clinging to the insides of my cheeks, nestling in the crevices between my teeth.

As though the wind had found its way into my stomach, it brewed a storm, clenched the walls of the braided-branch organ, and pushed up what had been just consumed. With a hand held to my mouth, I forced the pieces back down, but my body refused. And as though the wind carried by the people of Feng rushed to my aid by entering my body, it lifted every piece back up.

I stood and ran along the outer edge of the hall, past Grandmother, Aunt Xiangmu, and the others, past the people of Glace. The guards barely had time to react to my sudden appearance, pulling the doors out of the way just before I'd buried myself headfirst. I only made it several steps past the guards before I emptied the meat onto the floor. My eyes stung and my nose burned with sap and oil and blood.

This was worse than the journey to the markets. At least back then my stomach was more or less empty, and there wasn't a room filled with important individuals watching.

"Oh dear." Through blurry eyes, I saw Zinc roaming in the shadows, a cloak half white, half purple with elaborate designs adorning his back. "At least you didn't soil the dress." His casual tone made me want to laugh, but I felt far too sick.

I sucked in small breaths, willing my shaking to calm before speaking, and pushed myself from my hunched position. I had so many questions, but they were all whisked away from me as my head continued to spin.

"Why aren't you attending the ceremony?" I asked.

"Would you like me to be present?" He smiled, cocking his head to the side as if heartened by my question. "It seems you're having quite the rough time, huh?" Rather than the good-natured being I'd thought he was, there was a mocking edge to his question. Before I could respond, Grandmother's voice drifted from behind:

"Liu Lufeng."

She took slow strides towards me. Zinc had melted back into the shadows and vanished from sight.

"Grandmother." I swiped my lips with my cloak, adding to the stains already present. The taste of meat had lodged and made itself at home, even with the wind's attempts at expelling it.

Then, I corrected myself when I realized my mistake. "Elder." Grandmother frowned, disapproval knitting her forehead. "My apologies." I bowed, both for the informality and for fleeing the ceremony as I had.

Grandmother heaved a deep breath. "It is all right. Your mother fared little better." A small, melancholic smile.

"Why did you attend Mother's ceremony and mine, but not my other sisters'?" I asked.

"Ah, like your mother, you are the one most rooted in Feng. You must know that between you and your sisters, you value our traditions in Feng much more."

I thought about my sisters and the way they often spoke about leaving Feng, to become a princess of the Palace, to see what the world held outside of forests and rivers. They gauged one another's reactions, and though playful in their comments, underlying desire always laced their words—a growing envy for Mother after she left as they believed she was living a much better life in the Palace. To them, becoming Queen was far more glorious than becoming a weathered Elder.

"Yet I'm supposed to let it all go?" I finally said. My stomach continued to churn.

"In appearance, for now, you must."

"When will it end?"

Grandmother took my hand in hers. "That will be up to you to decide."

"And if I decide I want to stop now, return to Feng with you, can I?"

Her expression wilted, pitying, as she shook her head. "Not yet."

"Then when?"

"Lady Liu." Copper.

She took small, quick steps through the doors of the hall towards us. "Everyone is waiting on you and the Elder to continue the ceremony. It would be wise to return soon."

Grandmother bowed. "Apologies for my grand-daughter's sudden actions."

I followed suit. "My apologies."

"Oh, there is no need. It is an honor having both of you here with us." Copper flashed her teeth, tone high-pitched and sweet. "Now, shall we?"

Grandmother and I followed Copper back into the hall. I tried to keep my eyes on my empty chair rather than the many stares following us as we walked across the room. My steps echoed in the uncomfortable heeled shoes, the clacking thunderous.

When we returned to our seats, the Taskers had already cleared all the plates and cutlery and placed new porcelain plates in front of me and the King. The deer skull remained, glaring with empty sockets. In the place of the knife and fork were small metal grabbing tools with smooth, dull edges. My inability to maintain my calm had ruined my only opportunity. Sap burned, but I swallowed it down. There had to be another way.

I rushed to form a new plan while the Taskers set up the ritual table. I regarded the bone blade. It seemed more fitting for the King's death. To kill him just when he believed he'd won. My panic subsided, slightly, until the deer skull refocused in front of me.

Our Taskers situated themselves in front of us with a tool resembling the knife but with a bulky handle attached. With the press of a button, the blade began rotating. I held back the need to cover my mouth as they brought the blade down in the center of the skull, slicing clean through the bone from the front to the back. With gloved hands, the Taskers pulled it open.

Within the skull sat the deer's heart.

I imagined the bloody organ was still pulsing, the veins filled. A sob pried itself from my throat, but I snapped my mouth shut fast, pinching my lower lip between my teeth hard enough for sap to pool within.

The King dissected his heart with careful cuts before consuming a piece from the innermost layer. When I mimicked his actions, it wasn't as smooth. Every cut felt as though I were severing my own limb, piercing through my own bark, and a splatter of blood sprayed towards me, covering my cloak and dress in red speckles. The King lowered a finger, swiped it across the crimson of his plate, and placed it in his mouth, then reached over with a cloth and dabbed at my face before I could shrink away.

His gentle yet sickening act triggered my desire to flee again, but I remained firm in my seat and drove my fork into the piece, placing it in my mouth and swallowing with my gaze fixed on the deer skull.

This time, it didn't come back up.

The Taskers removed the decadent dessert made from Clay and Glace ingredients—a foamy slice of cake with heavy cream layers and pieces of cactus pear hidden between. I'd taken a bite, but even its sweet richness didn't entice my appetite to return after the deer.

The King raised his refilled cup, droplets of scarlet falling—red blossoming flowers on white cloth—and stood. A quiet fell over the hall. Reluctantly, I lifted my chalice, a numb and mechanical movement.

"To Feng and the Wind Walkers," he said.

A chorus repeated after him, the sound rising towards the domed ceiling. Grandmother stared solemnly at the King. She refused to meet my eye though I continued to will it.

"To the Palace and the Land Wanderers." Again, the echoes resounded. "To our friends who have travelled far—the Desert Treaders of Clay and the Water Shifters of Glace." He abruptly gazed at me. "To unity." He brought his chalice towards mine, nudging the cups together.

In slow motion, I brought the wine to my lips, offered the illusion of taking a drink with the tilt of my chin, but no wine entered. My mind remained firm on the King's death. There would be no further mishaps or distractions.

As he settled back in his seat, he leaned over and whispered, in Breath, "To family." A disgraceful use of the language.

My grip tightened around my chalice. I regretted allowing the Tasker to take away the knife. I would've used it to take the King's tongue, silencing him the way he'd silenced us all. There would be no elegance to his pitiful death.

"Allow me," he said with false chivalry as he loosened my fingers around the chalice. My toes curled.

The King stood, and with the sweep of his arm, he offered his hand to me. I followed, feet prickling with numbness, and placed my hand on his, barely touching. He led me towards the ritual table and waited for me to kneel in front of the sharpened bone blade before he took the same position across, in front of the jar of dark liquid and pen. His Tasker placed a scroll in the middle of the table and unrolled it with one hand, flattening it with his palm, fingers of rippling water—a Water Shifter from Glace.

Small intersecting lines and symbols, none of which I could understand, covered the parchment in neat rows. At the bottom was a waiting space. The King picked up the feather and dipped it into the jar before placing it against the parchment, drawing an unidentifiable scrawl, then he set the feather back down. I stared hard at the garble in front of me, willing comprehension, but it didn't matter, because I refused to complete the agreement.

I picked up the knife, and it trembled in my hand. This was my one chance. Praying to the wind to guide my thrust, I lunged forward to strike deep and hard into his ribs. But with a move as quick as the swirling tornados of the storm trees, he covered us from sight with his cloak and caught the knife in his hand before the blade could reach his body. My eyes widened when what poured from the wound was not blood but amber sap. He made a slight cough. My gaze met his. He tilted his head to the side, beckoning me to look past him. At the entrance, with the door slightly ajar, stood Chuiliu, frightened and confused, with guards right behind.

My breathing halted. The wind left me, sucked from both within my body and the surrounding air. No. No, no, no. My resolve shook at Chuiliu's presence. They'd brought her here to ensure I signed the agreement.

The desire to revolt simmered, then waned. My grip around the knife loosened, and the King released the blade, wiping his hand on the interior of his cloak before smoothing it out once more. My anger was replaced with the desperation to protect Chuiliu. I couldn't risk my sister's life for my impulsive desire for bloodshed. If I killed the King, maybe the guards would kill Chuiliu. They might also kill Grandmother, Aunt Xiangmu, and the others from Feng. I was a fool.

The agreement sat in front of me, and all I saw now was its reality—a thin slice of our dead. In silence, I mourned. There was no choice but to agree to the King's terms, even if the unknowable seemed worse than death.

My actions became mechanical as I slit my finger with the blade.

Always the guided, Sangshu's voice whispered in my mind.

I pushed the thought away and watched the amber sap well, along with my longing for Chuiliu, Mother, my family, before pressing down against the parchment.

I lifted my finger, agreement completed. The door to the hall closed once more. Chuiliu was gone. I only hoped they would return her to Feng, but I could never be sure. I promised to search the Palace later, in case they kept her as a prisoner. And if they did, I would break her out, agreement or not.

As we stood, my legs still quaking, threatening to drop me to my knees, my Tasker shuffled over with a folded white embroidered cloak in hand. Then I realized the King's 'kindness' in allowing me to wear Feng's cloak to the ceremony was not to respect my wishes nor my people's but to strip the cloak from me in front of everyone.

The King's Tasker pulled my cloak off, leaving my shoulders empty—but they'd never felt heavier. I recoiled from the stark white cloak with red and gold embroidery—like Copper's but even more magnificent and intricate—that the King's Tasker was fitting over me, but that was when I noticed he was only using a single arm, the other hidden, unseen.

"It will be okay." The whisper was so quiet I almost missed it, and as quick as it came, it disappeared along with the King's Tasker as he resumed his position.

I clutched at the new cloak from the inside, the silk smooth and slippery under my clammy grip. It was beautiful, but it also felt cold and suffocating, forcing my breaths to quicken, become shallow. I missed the cloak from Feng, even stained, even weathered.

The King's Tasker re-rolled the scroll. The King rose, eyes meeting mine once more before he turned to signal for the rest of the room to stand.

He held his right hand toward me, palm facing sideways, thumb pointing up, and waited. His eyes flitted to my hand concealed under my cloak. I mimicked his actions, extending my hand towards him. He took it in his, our hands interlocking. I followed. Then, he let go.

From behind me came a whisper from my Tasker: *A handshake. A customary gesture.*

The King looked around, then bowed. "Thank you all for gathering here today. We hope to welcome you again soon."

I winced at the thought of another gathering. I hoped it wouldn't be Chuiliu's wedding.

Everyone else bowed. Beginning with those closest to the door, one by one the guests leaked out of the hall. Panic welled within me as the people of Feng trickled out, until there was only Grandmother left. I hoped she would look back—she didn't. And I hoped to glimpse Chuiliu outside—I didn't.

I pushed back the feeling of loneliness, of the void their exit left.

Mother, where are you?

THE AGREEMENT

9

My fingers dug into my palm, and I bit back the pain caused by the taste of the meat. It was strange and foreign—yet enticing. Though it was sickness that lingered in my mind and stomach upon the first tasting—the way it both churned, sloshing like swamp water, yet warmed like gentle noon sun—the tip of my tongue abandoned my initial hatred: a feared craving and betrayed will. I thought of Grandmother, and I thought of Feng, and I swallowed the saliva pooling under and over my tongue from the thought of the meat—smoked fineness more delicious than sunlight, and sweet aged liquid of grapes more decadent than fresh river water. My stomach's original protestation allowed for what remained of the meat and its juices to settle, marinate within.

I wanted to fall to my knees and cry. The attachment

to my people, our connection, felt weakened by the ceremony. The independence I'd claimed in the moons prior to now felt like walls that were strong on the surface yet had rot and decay resting beneath. I held my ground, not wanting to give the King the satisfaction of knowing he'd cracked my resolve. I didn't want to think I'd failed to protect Chuiliu, but deep down, I knew I had.

"I hope the feast and ceremony was to your liking."

I wanted to scoff.

I wasted no time on undesirable small talk. "What was written in the agreement?"

He looked as though he expected the question and offered a somber nod. "Follow me."

Behind us, the two Taskers trailed. My Tasker now shadowed the King, and his own Tasker was at my heel.

"From now on, my Tasker, Geyser, will be at your aid. Tin here will still serve you when Geyser isn't present."

My Tasker. Tin. I tried her name in my mind, whispered it aloud; it felt strange on my tongue, though welcome, as it somehow made me feel closer to her. Tin didn't look too delighted by the arrangement, though she tried her best to mask it. Geyser seemed older than I was, but not by much. If he felt my gaze, he didn't offer a reaction.

"Where are we going?" I asked when we rounded a corner.

"My chamber," he said.

I hated that I continued to be led, to be brought from place to place, living moon by moon according to the agendas of others. Just like Sangshu said. Just like Yunshu and Heshi had always known—what I always denied.

The thought of soon being left alone with King caused my limbs to stiffen. Each step forward pained me. I drew my new cloak closer around me.

Up ahead was the hallway where the King's room awaited. My throat dried. I would rather flee through the window. When we entered the hall, I felt the urge to knock on every single one once more, particularly the door without a portrait, one I suspect now more than ever sat here waiting for Chuiliu's arrival, especially now that I was unsure of her whereabouts.

The King's door was without a handle and slid open of its own accord, the sound of bone on bone, as though pushed open by an unseen hand.

The interior was not grand, nor was it well lit, almost like a rectangular cave whittled and sanded. In the middle of the space was a long bone table with several seats made of the same material. The window was closed. A large metal box sat in the farthest corner with tangled metal vines protruding from its body.

The Taskers dragged out chairs for us both. When we were both seated, the King leaned forward with his elbows on the table, fingers laced beneath his chin.

"Why are we in here?" My tone was tight, sharp, as I bit out the words.

"Because we need to discuss."

"Discuss?"

He nodded, expression blank, yet there was a glint of eagerness—underlying excitement.

"Do you know why we were," the King asked, "*married*?" His tone disgusted me.

Behind the King, Tin was trying not to meet my eyes.

"To halt expansions on our land." To give me the chance to kill him, even though I'd failed; to find my family, to protect Chuiliu. "So we may keep our home, our people, our culture—intact."

He jutted his lips forward. "Is that what they told you? Your aunt? And your Elder?"

"Yes," I said.

"Well, I suppose that is partially true, though perhaps they thought you might be less resistant, more likely to cooperate, if they didn't tell you everything—like they did with your mother. Your sisters had already guessed most of it by the time the ceremonies came." The King motioned Geyser forward. In the Tasker's arm were a stack of bound papers, some thick, some slim. "Books," the King explained. "Geyser will teach you the basics, and Tin will help with the more advanced training, if you choose to undergo it, of course."

His words swam in my head, nonsensical. *Advanced training*. The King sensed my confusion.

"What we are," he pointed to himself, then to me,

"is 'business partners.' Feng only calls the ceremony a wedding, our relationship a marriage, because your Elder knows of no other sorts of relationships, of contractual relationships—or rather, won't accept them. This was the only way to negotiate with your Elder." I grimaced at his words, his attempts at turning the blame onto Grandmother, yet Grandmother was no better, to accept such an arrangement.

He sighed, then looked past me. I turned, following his gaze. There was a portrait of Mother—one that looked exactly like the photograph Zinc had given me. I shuddered at the image of her potential confinement, shrouded in darkness, away from the sun. "With your mother, that was a true marriage—at least, the one we had in Feng. The Elder was happy for us, until I left for the Palace. Unlike you, I had a choice, though now…"

He answered my question before I could ask: "I am your father. And yes, I only have one queen: your mother."

My temples throbbed, and my vision, usually sharp, blurred. My hands flew to the ring settled between my collarbones.

"Your mother was stubborn, still is, and your grandmother refused change. She pitied me because I chose the Palace, saying I should've been happy with what I have—had."

There was fleeting delight that tremored through me. Mother is alive. But I soon processed the rest of his words which reminded me of what those who left Feng had said to Grandmother. I kneaded at my eyes with my palms. Initial relief faded to sorrow as sap threatened to pour, and my voice rose as the first drop spilled.

"And why weren't you?"

I gave up hiding my tears. I wanted him to know my anger. I wanted him to feel regret. But his expression was almost too calm, sympathetic for only a moment before it became indifferent. To me, he would never be a father. My memory of him was near nonexistent, my imagination unable to conjure the potential family I could've had.

Then I remembered Grandmother's words: *He is dead. He died a long time ago.*

And truly, he had. He had decided to kill one self to begin another.

To me, my sisters, Mother, Grandmother, and Aunt Xiangmu were enough. They were always enough. I longed for my family to be reunited. The thought of our celebrations of a new annual came to mind. The way we would always huddle, arms clasped, in a tight circle, whispering our gratitude to the gods, to the sun, to the moon, to the waters, before ending with the wind that had always been beside us—an unseen guide, a gentle protector. No matter our differences during every other moon of the annual, it was the one moon we felt at peace, the one moon we felt as one. The King took that from me.

Geyser walked over and placed the stack of books next to me.

"There's so little movement, growth, back in our home, Fengfeng," the King said. "I didn't leave you and your sisters behind without purpose. And I didn't steal away your mother without cause."

I winced at his use of the nickname. How dare he try for my sympathy now? My needle threads tugged at their roots; small pricks scattered across my scalp. He'd abandoned what he should've sacrificed his life to protect, the same way Mother had, the way Grandmother had, the way my sisters had—though perhaps they were more willing—and the way I had. I would not let Chuiliu do the same.

"Was it all a lie then? Were all of our sacrifices futile? Will Feng ever be spared?" My flurry of questions didn't surprise the King, and that made me angrier. The question I wanted answered most left me: "Why did you bring Chuiliu to the Palace?"

It felt like hours before either of us spoke again, but only moments had passed.

"Feng will continue to exist as it always has," the King began. "But look at the world, Fengfeng. People will leave, and they will continue leaving until there is no one left."

He avoided my last question.

The King sounded exactly like the builders, the ones who thought they knew better than Grandmother.

Though I'd not lived nearly as long as the King, I refused to let his words convince me to desert my home and my people. Perhaps not all was lost. Maybe I didn't have to continue to plot his death; maybe I could change his mind, and maybe he might finally come home—but did I want that? I loathed the being in front of me and couldn't fathom ever thinking of him as my father. He'd done far more harm than he'd protected. Yet this might be the only way.

"Have you ever thought about returning to Feng?" I watched for regret, remorse, guilt.

The King was melancholic. A faraway expression aged him. "Sometimes," he admitted. "But I can't return." He stared at his smooth hands, as though he was seeing them for the first time.

"You can always return, if you choose to." At that moment, I wanted to take the King's hand in mine, but the rage at both his withheld secrets, and Grandmother's, boiled within me. The being in front of me was still but a missing shadow, a being that was never there—to convince myself otherwise now seemed an impossible task.

He dropped his hands back onto the table and shook his head. "There's no place for me now in Feng. I'm needed here. Far more than I'm needed at… home."

The thought of Grandmother overseeing Feng caused my own rough hands to quiver. She only had Chuiliu left. The King had taken everything from her. 'Home' was such an odd word coming from his mouth, even more so in reference to Feng.

"Lufeng. I gave up almost everything to come here—there's no return."

"And what about Grandmother?" Sap droplets collected between my clenched fists. The King remained silent.

I'd forgotten Geyser's and Tin's presence in the room. When I finally noticed them again, Tin was calm. So much so it frustrated me. Geyser looked away, as though feeling like an intruder.

"Did you know?" I fixed Tin with an accusatory gaze. She flinched and withdrew into herself as though I'd struck her.

With her shoulders hunched, cheeks pale, she said, "Yes."

"Where's Mother? And my sisters?" I addressed the King, thinking of the photographs from Zinc. I swallowed the taste of betrayal, of Grandmother having knowledge about this 'marriage', of my father sitting in front of me and pretending for annuals he wasn't related to us. I couldn't tell which was worse, the former or the latter, even if Grandmother's intentions for both had been to protect.

For a second, I recalled the photograph of the unknown Wind Walker I thought had been included by mistake. I imagined the King as the kind being, when he looked as though he could be my father, a time when he belonged to the wind. Except now, pity would be the best description of the expression he held. But then his features warped into one slow and cautious.

"You'll meet with them again," he said. "We'll have another dinner at a different palace, and your sisters will be present."

"Which sisters? And Mother?" I asked. "Chuiliu?"

"Patience, Fengfeng." His harsh eyes softened.

I wished to have nothing to do with him. But for now, I must keep him close, for he was the key to the lives of my family, and my only hope for escape. Suddenly, a thought shook me. Had my plot to kill the King not failed, would I have been regretful, having unknowingly jeopardized any opportunity for us to reconcile, even as impossible as the idea seemed now?

Though I still despised him and all he represented, by sap and roots, he was still my father. Grandmother would've wanted me to call him Father. Sometimes sap was stronger than betrayal. At least for us, even if Father seemed as though he was from the Palace, I was certain roots remained.

Once I'd imagined running away, hiding in the densest areas of Feng, so Chuiliu would be trained to become the next Elder instead. I wasn't like Grandmother, who was fearless in her ability to deal with others, to be able to manipulate them so effortlessly, or at least more so in the past; or like Mother, who had the gentlest of souls, lending anyone a resting shoulder and listening ear; or

Chuiliu—though she was still young, she already had a fire brewing within her, stronger than all of her sisters, reminding me most of Sangshu. The youngling only needed time to unlock it. My rebellion, my courage, and my ambition to kill the King had all been smothered in an instant, reverting me back to who I was, who I am. All the fury driven by my previous desperation waned faster than light during long and harsh winters.

I didn't want to become like the King, to be so detached from Feng, to become so settled, *comfortable* and *content* in this unnatural place. But it seemed like I would have to. I'd signed an agreement, after all— and I understood that what had been signed by blood, by sap, by whatever ran through the veins, was an unbreakable oath.

Yet the need to rebel, to break the agreement, simmered within me. I would find a way to escape, and when I did, it would be with my family—Mother, my sisters, with or without Father. I allowed the yearning thoughts of home to carry me out of the King's chamber. Though I had not the King's sap on my hands, I would use his own words against him.

It had been three nights since the ceremony, and I wasn't anywhere near thinking up an appropriate plan for escape.

I walked down the empty corridors. My breath came

in shallow currents until I arrived back in the hallway of my family's rooms. I recalled the blocked-off wall—the existence of another side of the Palace inaccessible, and wondered if Mother and Chuiliu might be there.

Though recalling the photograph, Mother might well still be in the room with her portrait. I hastened down the hall, lingering only a few moments on each portrait before stopping in front of Mother's door. Perhaps this time...

I pressed my lips against the sliver where the door met the frame and whispered, "Mother?" hoping the wind might somehow carry my words through like it did back in Feng.

Silence.

I tried again. "Mother?"

I wanted to pound against the door, demand someone open it for me, but I knew I would only be whisked away and placed back in my room. I gathered up another breath, hoping to make a third attempt, but the word died upon my lips. I backed away. Perhaps she wasn't here after all. There'd been no answer the first time I'd knocked when I discovered this hall—it seemed foolish of me to believe that it'd be otherwise now.

Just as I was about to leave, a low gust of wind brushed my ankles. It tingled the bottoms of my feet through the silk fabric shoes I now barely noticed I wore, much like how I unconsciously folded the sheets and fluffed my pillow after waking each morning on the newly made nest on the floor—actions I would've never performed back in Feng.

The door to the room with Mother's portrait slid open. Before I could hesitate, I burrowed into the darkness, and the door closed behind me.

In the dark, a light flickered on, adjusted by slim fingers so the glow was dim rather than blinding. Next to the lantern was Mother, rocking gently on a chair made of bone. By her feet was a small, wide urn, filled to the brim with soil.

The desperation of the choked third attempt welled up my throat, and this time, it escaped. "Mother." Then again, with more urgency—a mixture of joy and fear, an intermingling of seasons brewed within me. "Mother! Alive— You— We need to go; we need to leave. Return home together. We can—"

She raised a hand, placed a finger against her lips. I had no plan, but I hoped for her escape. Now that I'd found her, I swore never to lose sight of her again.

Her ghostly smile held only a fragment of the warmth I remembered, as dim as the light next to her, one that might flicker and extinguish if it met the lightest breeze. The smile differed from the one in the photograph— strained, tired, defeated. Upon her shoulders was draped a white cloak with embroidered patterns similar to my own, a design Zinc likely customized.

The grooves of age had plunged further into her face, along her arms and frail feet. No longer were the needle threads on her head a deep earthy brown mixed with the Feng forests' green, but dots of white moss speckled along their untrimmed length, bundled at the nape. She'd gotten little sunlight.

If I could, I would've pulled her back to my room and ripped open the curtains, streaming into the room the warmth of the sun. If I knew how, I would've healed her worries, her wounds.

We all knew what happened if we strayed from the wind, away from light, for too long.

We would wither.

Perhaps that was why all those who left did not return—they couldn't. And though our people were many, with the current direction of migration, our number would soon dwindle. *Was it worth it?* I wanted to ask them all.

"Fengfeng." Though I hadn't heard the nickname from Mother's lips for many annuals, the feeling of security it gave me was a gentle caress. It held such a different tone to Father's, who desired reconnection, but the distance between us was a yawning chasm.

My name from Mother's lips was a cry of longing, of melancholic nostalgia, of a yearning for home. It reminded me that we were each other's homes. And even though she'd left us to follow her first love, in hope of change, I forgave her in the way I could never forgive Father.

"I thought you were—" I didn't allow the morbid words to escape me.

She nodded, slow, and sighed. "Sangshu believed the same." I recalled my sister's harsh words and remembered my desire to prove her wrong.

The room was simple, the bed not nearly as extravagant as the one I had, nor was the décor.

"Why have they kept you in this room?" I asked.

She smoothed down the white, red, and gold dress she had on. "To control your father," she said, "so he wouldn't do anything rash or go against those he works for. The Palace owners."

Why did Father not say he was under the control of others? Did I seem too weak for the truth? Incapable? Then, I wilted at the thought. Perhaps I truly was.

"I thought—"

"No, your father doesn't own the Palace. There are people far more powerful than he is. People you will soon meet." Her expression was grim, her words a warning.

I noticed only now that Tin had never referenced the King when she spoke of permissions and the like—I'd only assumed.

"The wind has been carrying me word of your arrival, the ceremony, among other things." She drew a deep breath. "But I couldn't reveal myself. It was too much of a risk."

Her words made me realize how the creators of the Palace wanted us to feel free yet constantly reminded us that we were only free because they had allowed our freedom. Mother could open her own door, yet she could never leave her room. I could roam the halls, yet I couldn't ever step out the gates unchaperoned.

I was about to throw myself into her lap when she held up a hand, drawing my attention back to the bundle at the crook of her elbow. "Changqing," she whispered, peeling back the white cotton to reveal a small face. "Your brother."

A child.

I dropped to my knees in front of her.

The saplings of Feng did not cry, not like the Land Wanderer and Desert Treader children carried on the backs of some at the markets. Instead, our children rustled, like leaves in the wind, shivering when scared, when in need, when sad, when desiring love until they reached ten annuals.

"How?" I asked.

She nudged the urn that held soil from Feng. "It wasn't easy to sneak in." Mother looked back at Changqing.

"When?" I moved closer, marveling at the curve of Changqing's nose, his closed eyes, his smooth bark with sealed fractures that would split open and deepen as he aged. The growth of our physical body stalled at twenty annuals, but we could always tell age by the crevices in our bark, the withering of our roots and needle threads, the spots that appeared over time on our branches. I wondered if he was already contracted to work for the Palace, if they forced such an agreement on Mother.

"Just after Sangshu's ceremony," she said. "Geyser

was a great help. Yunshu and Heshi never visited or tried to find me." Her forehead creased further.

"Maybe they thought—" I began, again allowing my thoughts to trail.

"No. They knew I was alive. But they couldn't resist. Not like you and Sangshu."

I wasn't surprised, just disappointed. "Not like you," I said finally.

"More like your father," she said with a sad smile. "I can't blame them."

I thought of the cakes, of the meat and its strange yet addictive taste, of the shoes on my feet, the soft cloak on my shoulders, the comfort of the bed—

"What would happen if we broke the contract? Fled? Hid?"

Her smile was the drooping stem of a riverweed scorched by the sun, unseen by the rain for too many moons. "Death." She paused. "Not for us, but for Feng. Though we'd likely be found quickly and brought to the prison in Engine, like Sangshu, though she was able to escape."

"Engine?" I asked, then, "Sangshu?" Then—

Escape. Escape was a possibility. Someone was successful, and perhaps I could be too.

Mother rose from her chair and moved towards thick black velvet cloths I now knew were called curtains. Bleak light flooded the room, muting the warmth of the lantern. The sun was blotted by dense clouds, something rare to Feng's clear skies. Mother pried open the window, and the scent hit me first—a strange metallic smell, something denser, more nauseating than the oil massaged into meats, than the Travelers—air that was impure, stale, thick and mind-dizzying.

I moved to stand behind Mother and Changqing by the window, thoughts of Sangshu's cunning running through my mind before they were interrupted by the sight.

Staring outwards, I realized the wall encasing the Palace literally cut through the middle, limiting access to the sides, separating Feng from the rest of the world.

"Over there is Gear, and past it is Engine."

Below the Palace was water, a mass so dense and endless, I wondered if reaching the bottom was possible. Beyond the stretch of waves were large sculpted grey stones lined in neat rows. Protruding from the top of each were smooth cones, pumping out smog. Between them stood what appeared to be large wheels powered by water. Past the endless stretch of what Mother described as factories and electricity towers that made up Gear sat Engine. I had heard the Travelers described using this same word. Engine was fitting of its name and resembled as such, with bridges that extended outwards like arms, clasping onto Gear to connect the two. The lights from Engine pulsed with unnatural colors, too bright. These shades were similar to the pigments that lined Zinc's features and those used in the Glace artisans' glasswork.

"We're trying to get him out—your father and I. To

give Changqing a choice." She glanced at the door. "You have another brother. Older than you only by three annuals. But he was not birthed the natural way. I'm not sure where he is now. They took him for the experiments."

It couldn't be.

She brushed the fine needle threads of Changqing with her fingers. "Geming is his name. *Revolution*. I was optimistic that, maybe, he could drive the change. I was so hopeful when he was born… The Palace isn't a great place for that, is it? Hope, I mean." She smiled sadly as she caressed my brother's cheek.

The image of the being dripping in blue-green shifting water, borrowing wind, rattled within my mind. At least he was alive, but knowing this fact might only add to her worries.

The resemblance now made sense. I had to speak to Geming again. But to do so I would trigger the alarms and have him tumble once again out of the metal chamber. That didn't seem safe for either of us.

I reached towards Changqing. He curled his small fingers around mine. I shook within his light grasp. He sensed the shift in mood. His smile waned. I relaxed, allowing the gentleness of his touch to calm me, hoping his smile would return. It didn't.

There was something else Mother stopped herself from saying. That Changqing was in danger. That perhaps we might suffer the same fate as Geming.

A cold sliver shot down my spine. I tried to

estimate the distance between the Palace and Engine. Immeasurable. My hope plummeted. I felt like a flower ripped from its stem. Mother's hand caressing my jaw cleared my mind of worries, but the calm lasted only a second as footsteps approached.

Mother's voice was tight, feverish as she clutched Changqing. "Go!"

"But—"

Mother pulled out a small glass square the size of my palm from her cloak.

"A photograph?" I asked, although the glass was blank.

Mother shook her head quickly. "A comscreen."

"How do you use it?"

"There's no time for that now," Mother said. "Keep it safe. No one should see it. Sangshu will send a message when she can. They're searching for her still, hopefully she hasn't yet been found."

At the mention of Sangshu's name, my first thought was again her hurtful message and the questioning of my position as eldest. I couldn't blame her. I wasn't the mountain my sisters could depend on.

Mother placed her hand over mine.

"Remember this. Language is a double-edged sword, but fear not, Fengfeng. You'll know what you need to do."

I didn't feel as though I would, but I nodded, trembling.

"You must go now, before someone realizes you are here. Tell no one about Changqing."

I wondered how long it had been since she'd seen Father, even if their rooms were next to one another's.

When I left Mother, I felt suddenly cold. The lingering image of smog-dominated Gear and Engine invaded my thoughts, battling against the naïve face of Changqing. With my family scattered, I wanted to reclaim the choice that was taken from us all and ensure my brother could choose when and where he might make his home. I brushed my hand across the outline of Mother's portrait. The smooth strokes made her look so much younger.

My mind flicked back to the cold metal chamber that held Geming, and I imagined the faces of each family member peeking from the glass, trapped, experimented on, becoming something other than themselves. Not just Mother and Chuiliu; now I had to get my brothers out of the Palace, too—if it wasn't already too late for Geming.

10

GEAR AND ENGINE

We began my studies a few moons later. Geyser turned out to be an annoyingly excellent teacher—one with a gentle voice and the patience of the gods.

I didn't want to learn the Palace's written language, but I knew I must so I could read the agreement and understand what I'd committed to, read their books to better understand the world of Land Wanderers. Like Mother said, languages, words, were truly powerful things.

That could be the reason most of those living in Feng had been prevented from learning it, limited only to spoken Script. It was to keep us under control, from speaking out, from rebelling—at least until we signed an agreement, a contract, in ignorance, forcing us to become docile and useful. It baffled me to think that perhaps

Grandmother knew of the details of the agreements yet left most of Feng in the dark. Aunt Xiangmu, too, having always been the one present during the negotiations. Or maybe the Land Wanderers had forbidden them to speak about it all. I'd thought little about how the two could read and write Script and understood it only as something necessary given their positions in Feng.

The symbols, images, on the contract at the ceremony were letters, as Geyser described. My mind conjured the image of Mother and my sisters practicing their writing on endless sheets of paper, on the dead, marring their already mutilated bodies.

"This is written Script," Geyser explained. Glace used another oral form—Song—but for the people of the Palace, those from Clay, and those who lived on the other side of the wall, Script was the language they shared.

I thought of Feng's carvings, temporary rather than permanent, the way we committed our histories to memory instead of through text.

It was strange seeing my name written out in an unfamiliar form. Geyser guided me through each stroke, though the letters appeared clumsy, crooked. His translucent fingers looked as though they might feel similar to the cool waters of Feng rivers, but they felt warm, like tree trunks soaked in the noon sun and mellowed near sundown.

After hours, my writing had improved little, and my hand ached, the joints stiff. Compared to Geyser's elegant calligraphy, mine resembled a forest creature's random markings on a tree.

"It gets easier," he said. "It was hard for me, too, at first."

"And Tin?"

For a moment, he refused to meet my prodding stare before admitting that Tin could neither read nor write, and I wondered if she'd been limited by those more powerful than Father, so she could be easily controlled.

Unlike the others in the Palace, I felt unusually close to Geyser, and perhaps it was because Mother mentioned he'd helped her. I wished he was my older sibling. Or perhaps this only revealed my desire to run from the responsibilities as the eldest—albeit that was no longer so, now I had discovered Geming's existence.

Geyser checked the door, listening for sound outside, before returning to me, leaning down and whispering, "Back in Glace, we didn't need to speak to one another, at least not verbally, not like this. We'd gather by the water, dip our fingers in"—he held up three fingers, twirled them in the air—"and allow the rhythm of the water, its currents, its flow, to carry the words to each other."

Much like the wind.

Geyser smiled at the memory, then dropped his hand.

"It feels more intimate than the spoken language," he said.

I agreed, thinking about how it felt to listen to words carried by and through the wind rather than the limited echoes of the sounds Geyser and I were currently sharing.

"Hold on to it," Geyser said. I knew he meant the wind.

Unlike Father, Geyser seemed kind, honest, and though he wasn't from Feng, he reminded me of home.

Even after seven moons passed, I made little progress.

The textbooks beside me held information about Gear and Engine. I itched to read the words hidden between the pages. Maybe they would offer me information I needed to find Sangshu.

"Time." Geyser smiled, reassuring. "It takes time."

Geyser brought me tea while I worked, which I appreciated, and I found myself relishing the comfort of his company, having spent most of my time alone in my room prior to the ceremony.

I scribbled my name yet again, sighing when I compared it to his example at the top of the sheet. It was much easier reading the words than trying to replicate them.

Sensing my frustration, Geyser had another Tasker bring in a contraption called the Typer with a series of oval keys with Script inscribed on them. Though it was difficult to remember the location of each letter, I imagined it was far preferable using this than the quill. He fed it with paper and ink and told me I could test the keys as I marveled at the strange machine. Given what Zinc had previously mentioned about more advanced technology, I wondered what could be even more convenient than the Typer.

By the end of the cycle, I found it much easier to mimic his written words, abandoning the Typer out of stubbornness alone. I guided my hand in creating the foreign letters with greater ease and recognized words we'd been going over, though I still stumbled and relied heavily on the Word Searcher.

"You'll soon be running one of the palaces or perhaps somewhere in Gear and Engine. You'll need to understand the workings of contracts." Geyser gestured to the texts in front of us, always with his right hand, never his left. When the left side of his robe fluttered upwards, carried by an incoming breeze from the window, I saw only air. I recalled how he performed his duties as a Tasker all with a single hand, though I never thought much of it until now.

While Geyser was not looking, I took the liberty of skimming ahead in our lessons, seeking familiar words. I searched for the word 'experiment'. There was no information, but I was sure they must've kept it hidden somewhere in the Palace.

I was wary about the feeling of the pages between my fingers; I tried my best to suppress the thought.

Within one text, there was a current report of the situation in Gear:

In Gear, Wind Walkers and Water Shifters work in harmony with the Land Wanderers and Desert Treaders within factories, ensuring the smooth inner workings of the city of Engine.

Harmony. I wondered how true that was.

Engine is a vibrant city that will fulfill its citizens' wildest wishes. Browse the glorious selection of movies, shows, and subscribe to comvid with your family and friends! The online megashops are great for the latest deals and products!

I wasn't sure if this was how all textbooks were supposed to be, but the oral lessons passed on to us by Grandmother were nowhere near as informal as this. Descriptions of Gear and Engine felt far from the reality outside Mother's window. And though Engine was vibrant with its colors and technology, I feared its development, the way it might grow, conquer, destroy.

When Geyser left my room, I tore through the books with a Word Searcher in hand over the next few moons. It'd become much easier for me to read the foreign texts, but there were still many words I didn't know. Each time I stumbled across one unfamiliar, I'd commit it to memory until my reliance on the Word Searcher lessened.

But the more I flipped through the texts, the more confused I became. Every word and sentence strived to make the Palaces, Gear, Engine, appear like heavenly places. They were not. Yet I found the words were swaying me.

I put down the texts and struggled to remind myself why I was learning Script. Not for Father or Copper, nor the Palace, but for Mother and Changqing and Chuiliu.

Geyser returned for our lessons every moon, and after two cycles, I'd made more progress than both he and I expected, although it resulted in many sleepless nights and jittery mornings. Bean tea from Clay, I'd discovered, was far stronger than root tea, and kept me from the rest I couldn't afford.

"Your people have always had a gift for languages," he whispered, "much like my own." Geyser had a faraway expression as he brushed his fingers across my words.

I'd hoped we could speak again about the water and his life in Glace, but we hadn't, though I understood his caution, given how there seemed to be eyes and ears everywhere.

Geyser looked around, as if checking for intruders. Eagerness swelled within me in anticipation of what he might say. He remained silent and instead pulled out two large textbooks from his bag.

"I noticed your interest"—his eyes searched mine— "in learning more about the other side." Then he tapped his fingers against the books we'd been going through the past few moons. "Don't believe everything you read."

I didn't, but it was reassuring to hear that he, too, didn't believe all of what was written in these texts.

"I used to work in Gear," he said, before he headed for the door. I wondered about what he'd done and how he'd ended up here.

When I lifted one text to marvel at the intricate gold title, I frowned when I realized it was the same material as all the other books he'd had me read. I flipped it open anyhow, just to check, and it settled in the middle, where a space had been carved out in the pages, and there was a copper key. On it was an engraving that said *Library*—a place of knowledge, as Geyser had previously described.

I had read in one text that libraries in Engine altered their books to document only who they believed to be the key historical events and figures—their own. Though from what I recalled, it was from a page that didn't belong to the book, as though Geyser had specifically placed it there for me to find without alerting anyone else of its existence.

When I looked back up, Geyser was lingering by the entrance with a smile. He left the door slightly ajar and on the ground was a faint line of his damp footprints, the glistening in the dim light. I'd heard Water Shifters left remnants of themselves everywhere they went, but this was the first time I'd noticed. I knew I had to be quick before the steps disappeared altogether. Geyser was nowhere to be seen outside in the halls.

But the ghost of his footprints was what I followed.

∞

I worried about making it back to my room later without Geyser's steps to guide me, so I made a note of the paintings I passed, along with the different contraptions in the display cases, and their titles:

Alum Poten

Hair Groomer

Lotiana Kravinet

Air Waterer

And when the footsteps halted, a door with *Library* engraved on it stood in front of me.

Though Geyser had explained its uses, there was nowhere to insert the key, so I held it up, hoping some sort of crevice might open. To my surprise, the door slid to the side as soon as the body of the copper met its surface.

Inside, I expected Geyser to be present since his footprints had stopped at the entrance, but he was nowhere to be found. The room was lined with shelves. Texts, thin and thick, graced each divided section. A long table sat in the middle riddled with pieces of smooth parchment, along with glass photographs and comscreens. At its edge was a rolled document.

I recognized the broken seal that was still attached; peeking out from the slightly unraveled sheet was dried amber. The agreement.

I reached for the parchment, smoothing it out. At a frantic pace, I skimmed the contents, surprised at how it was once an incomprehensible mess of letters yet now I understood all that was written. It outlined my duties as a new business partner, some of which Geyser had already mentioned: the contracts, taking over one of the many palaces, taking up stations.

But there was a single line at the bottom that caused my legs to buckle, as I grasped the edge of the table for balance.

Liu Chuiliu shall be entered into the experiment in four months post signing of this agreement.

The experiment—the one Mother wanted to save Changqing from, the one Geming had undergone.

Four months. *Four cycles.*

I slammed a fist against the table. The papers rattled and crinkled under my bark.

There was less than half a cycle left from when I'd signed the agreement during the ceremony. I had to find Chuiliu.

The only relief I felt was that Changqing's name was absent. At least he remained a secret, for now.

On the table, there were images and words on paper that looked far more recent than the pages of the textbooks Geyser had given me to read. Images with large bold fonts popped up from the glass comscreens.

Clay's Purchase of Glace

**Looming Revolution in Engine Laborers
and Experimentation on Water Shifters
and Wind Walkers. Protests Underway.
At First Peaceful, Now Becoming Violent!**

A PALACE NEAR THE WIND

Innovation Thrives

Z INC. Continues to Rise!

**The New World of the Land Wanderers
Nearing Now!**

**Gear Factory Revolts Calmed
For Now**

Z Inc. It couldn't be. Given the dinner with Father and my sisters soon, I suspected I would find out the truth there, and if I didn't, I would prise it out of them.

Gear, Engine, maybe even Zinc, wanted to hide everything from us. At least on this side of the wall. Grandmother surely wouldn't stay so still if she knew what was really happening, how our people were being used. I rummaged through papers and glass that repeated the same information in different ways, some proclaiming everything was a tragedy, some glorifying the violence, some rooting for the rebellion, others cursing the rebellion and riots for stirring chaos.

On the floor, ripped in pieces, was what I was looking for: the documents about the experiments. With hunger, I read faster than the phrases could process in my mind, stumbling over unfamiliar words, then rereading them.

**Success rate of the experiments
increasing exponentially!**

**Become someone more, become
more than human, join
the evolution.**

**From 0.002%, the success rate
has now increased to 0.03%!**

**Synthetic Birthrates of Wind Walkers
and Water Shifters in Gear and
Engine up 10%–5% Higher
Than Last Year!**

"No," I whispered. Their intention to force Chuiliu into those cold chambers, submerged in liquid, was cruel. I thought of Geming, the wails of pain, the unnatural blue-green I'd found him in. *Become someone more.* Did the Land Wanderers wish to *become* us?

Mother would tell me that the agreement wasn't my fault, but it felt as though it was. I brought my hands to my face, pressing hard against my eyes, causing white clouds to swirl in my vision.

I'd thought the Land Wanderers wanted to convert us all. But no, what they wanted to do was steal all that made us who we were, use us then toss us away.

Hidden under the comscreens was a photograph of Sangshu. I realized the word on the photograph Zinc had given me said 'Wanted.' But in this picture, she looked energized, less haggard. I ran a finger over the text both above and below her image.

A PALACE NEAR THE WIND

They call her Contract Breaker.
"I know a way to escape them." —Sangshu

I left the documents as I found them, worried that someone might notice if I took any. I was now sure there must have been some sort of rebellion already, unspoken of, hidden, within this Palace, if Sangshu was able to escape. She couldn't have done it alone.

I thought of Geyser, the most likely of allies, given Mother's words, and the fact he'd shown me this library. I thought of the copper key, its specific material given everything else in the Palace was made of bone, and wondered what he was trying to hint at. Even if it were only a ruse to gain my trust, I had no choice but to trust him now.

Before I returned to my room, I needed to see Mother again to tell her what I had discovered about Chuiliu. As soon as I entered the King's hall, I heard the sound of scratching underneath one of the doors.

Chuiliu's door.

I pressed my ear against the bone, then slid down when I realized it was coming from the almost nonexistent opening beneath.

"Chuiliu?" I whispered, my voice strained, harsh, in an attempt to be both quiet and loud. More scratches. I scraped my nails against the ground in response.

"Fengfeng?" The voice was muffled, quivering in Breath, but it was unmistakably Chuiliu's.

"Are you okay? How long have you been in there?" I held my breath. I'd knocked on this very door after the wedding, but she must have not been placed there for there was no response. I'd been so focused on my studies I'd made no further attempts to check again. How foolish of me.

"Not long after the wedding." Her voice sounded strained, weary.

I hoped her room was not the same as Mother's, looking out into the dreariness of Gear.

"Can you open the door?" I pressed my face hard against the cold floor with a shudder.

"Yes, but—"

"Then open it!" I slapped my hand against the door in exasperation—not to scare her, but in my impatience to know she was unharmed and safe, or as safe as she could be here.

"He made me sign something," she said. "A Land Wanderer with colorful pigments smeared across his features." Zinc. "He said if I left the room, I'd get in trouble. Big trouble. That something bad will happen to me, and to you, to Feng."

To threaten such a youngling. I sneered at the thought of Zinc offering the power to escape but not the choice to use it. Had he told her anything else, about being placed in those wretched chambers? I wanted to ask, but I didn't want to frighten her more.

"It's okay," I said. "Open the door. You don't need to come out. I'll come in."

There was a whimper before the door slid open, slowly. I ran in, almost toppling Chuiliu over, just as she flung her arms around me. She felt smaller than before, even though it had been almost four cycles since I'd left. I buried my fingers in her needle threads. She smelled too much of the Palace's staleness; the scent of Feng had almost left her completely.

Unlike Mother's, Chuiliu's room wasn't barren. It was as extravagant as my own, with red and gold and white accents. A trick, an illusion built to entice Chuiliu, no doubt. But the bed looked untouched, the window shut to hide the sickening view of Gear and Engine. In the corner sat a blanket pooled in the shape of a small pond. I almost smiled, thinking back to my own floor nest.

"Will we be okay?" Chuiliu asked, her voice uneven.

"Yes." I was always lying to her. I wanted badly for it to be the truth, but I didn't know what would happen to us both if we remained here. To become like Father, so removed from our family and home, was a nightmare. "I have a plan," I said.

The Travelers. We could steal one, use it to flee back to Feng. I wished nothing more than to borrow the wind instead, but I couldn't outpace the Travelers.

"We can go home, together." My voice cracked when I thought back to the agreement, how I'd signed her life away.

We'd be safe as soon as we crossed the border, the boundary between Feng and the Palace where the stone path abruptly ended. Grandmother would protect us, she'd have to. Even if it wasn't part of any written agreement, all those who crossed into Feng were under the Elder's protection, unless they were malicious, unless they caused harm.

First, I would need to learn how to use a Traveler. They had a few on standby near the entrance of the Palace for the guards to use or for Tin and me when we went to the markets. I could steal one. It would be difficult to fit us both, but Chuiliu was small enough.

I thought of myself on top of a Traveler. Each harsh, uprooting step it would take towards Feng.

"Listen." I bent so our faces were level. "The next time I come, I'll need you to open the door right away, okay?"

"But we'll get in trouble—"

"We won't. We'll be gone before they notice. Now promise me you will," I said.

Chuiliu chewed on the inside of her cheek and was slow to dip her head, but eventually she was bobbing up and down vigorously.

"Here." I took off my jade necklace and guided it over Chuiliu's head. "Hold onto this for me until I come back."

Though she nodded again, I knew she was skeptical of my words. I also knew she would trust me. I hoped it wasn't something I'd break.

I gave her one last hug before I slipped out of her room.

THE DINNER

For the next few moons, I plotted my escape with Chuiliu. Though there were Travelers parked next to the entrance, there would be two guards stationed at each side of the door. Next to one of the guards, there was the button I'd seen them push to open the gates.

I had to find a way to distract the guards when I made my move, and it would have to be soon. Every moon that passed was a risk.

Maybe I could ask Tin to go to the markets again, so I could practice using the Traveler on my own, but before I could ring the bell to call her, the comscreen Mother gave me vibrated within the folds of my cloak. But by the time I'd settled myself enough to withdraw it, the comscreen had stopped vibrating.

With anxious and trembling hands, I gripped onto the glass and tapped the surface, but there was the symbol of a lock. When I pressed it, numbers and letters appeared on the screen—some sort of code I had to decipher. Mother had given me no hints. The thought that there might not be another call until it was too late sent shockwaves to my temples.

I almost jumped when the comscreen vibrated and lit up in my hands again. After almost dropping it, I stilled enough to focus on the text.

Trust no one, nothing, except for the songs of the terracotta dunes. I'm in hiding. Get to the other side of the wall, to Gear. I will find you. —Sangshu

Songs of the terracotta dunes? From her message, it seemed at least she was free. But how would I get to Gear, and how would I bring our family with me?

On the comscreen, a giant cross flashed, and when I tapped it, numbers ticked downward, the words wiping from the screen when it reached zero.

I hid the glass within my cloak, when a knock sounded at the door. The implications of my sister's warning but also her title in Engine swirled in my mind. *Contract Breaker.*

"Pardon me, Lady Liu," Tin said as she entered.

An uncomfortable expression then slipped onto her face. "The King would like to know if you might want some of the… same meats from the ceremony? He would ask for the Hunters to fetch them." Tin looked away. She didn't add that the hunting grounds would likely be the outskirts of Feng. An implied horror.

I silenced the words clawing up my throat. The sudden memory of the delicious spices and oils mixed with the strange, yet alluring taste of meat and smoke threatened to overwhelm me: *Yes.*

"No." I crossed my arms.

Tin reminded me that the dinner at the other palace was looming closer. The King must have wanted me to get used to consuming meat. I hoped it was nothing like what we'd had during the ceremony, yet I also wished deep down that it would be. Would I meet the owners of the palaces at this dinner?

"Was your name always Tin?" I asked as she turned to leave the room.

A hard smile appeared on her face. "No." But she said nothing further, and I didn't pry. Perhaps she'd forgotten her old name, or perhaps she simply didn't want to remember.

Before we left the Palace for the dinner, while I dressed myself in the Palace robes—something more muted, beige, rather than something brighter—Tin debriefed me:

"We'll be heading to the palace in Clay, the one run by your sister, Yunshu... She goes by Yena now."

"Yena?" I asked. It was not just the name that surprised me but also the fact that she ran a palace of her own. Though perhaps that should've been expected, given Father's rule over the one near Feng.

Tin paused. "Yes, and your sister Heshi, who will also be present, now goes by Harley."

It was unheard of in Feng to change our names after birth. Grandmother would be disappointed to hear about their abandonment. Unless she already knew. Though it was a surprise, a part of me had predicted this might happen.

"Will we be going by Traveler?" My stomach was already complaining at the thought, but this was the chance I was looking for.

"Unfortunately, yes. But only partway. Then we'll be travelling on something a bit," Tin struggled to find the right word, "sturdier."

"Will Geyser be coming with us?" I looked for the familiar figure but didn't notice him around.

"Unfortunately not," she said, apologetic, as I followed her towards the entrance. For a moment, I was disappointed, knowing his presence would help reassure me. But when we reached the gates, and I'd spotted the awaiting Travelers, my attention focused elsewhere.

"May I?" I gestured to the control panel.

Tin, surprised, placed her controller back in her cloak. I hopped into the already-lowered Traveler and tried to recall Tin's previous instructions. The symbols were a jumble in my head, but Tin was patient while she waited for me to bring the contraption to a jerky start.

At least this time I didn't vomit. It felt different with me controlling the machine. I knew the speed, I felt more connected to the steps, yet at the same time, I feared this familiarity.

Past the markets we visited the first time I left the Palace were the valleys and troughs of dunes turned from a dark beige to a brown that was almost... red. Was this what Sangshu was referencing? Perhaps she meant Yunshu given her home in Clay—perhaps Yunshu hadn't abandoned our home after all. Yet Mother said she had never come to seek her out.

The sand eventually smoothed out into a winding dark path—strange and uniform like the one between the Palace and Feng, but one dusted rather than pristine. It was made from a million rocks packed together, smooth rather than jagged.

The shift from the sinking sand onto the path wasn't unlike the shift from uneven soils onto the bone tiles of the Palace. I'd expected there to be other journeyers, yet we were alone. Waiting for us down the stretch of the path was something similar to a Traveler, but instead of legs it had six large rubber wheels, the middle rimmed with metal.

Three nestled on each side of an oblong half-shell, the same height as me. Above the shell, propped up by slim metal poles, was a dome shielding the inside from direct sun rays. At the tip, a translucent curtain pooled down—a waterfall of fabric reaching just before the wheels. In front of the machine was another small half-shell attached with its own dome. A Desert Treader sat behind a panel that resembled the one on Travelers.

"A Carrier," Tin said.

A small set of steps extended from the back of the Carrier like a tail. We dismounted from our Travelers, and Tin gestured for me to walk up. I headed up and pushed aside the curtain. The handles inside the Carrier were not made of bone but a compact grainy stone. Though the texture was rough, I much preferred it.

Behind, outside the shifting curtains, I noticed that the guards we arrived with remained to watch over our Travelers.

I expected the jerk and stumble in movement once the Carrier started, but other than a few bumpy trembles, the wheels turned smoothly across the pathway towards Clay. I wondered what Heshi's journey might be like, wherever she might have been travelling from, and I wondered if the machines and roads in Clay's palace were more elegant, or more natural, like Feng's. I'd heard from Geyser that Glace had waterfalls, as tall as, if not taller, than the Palace near Feng, and mountains that towered over the walls. I wondered what Clay's might hold. And I wondered if I would ever get to see Glace and hear the songs of its people that Geyser had told me of, and why the meeting was not held there instead. Song. Their language. Of course. That must've been what Sangshu was referencing. Perhaps that was why Geyser wasn't here. Perhaps the Palace owners already knew he couldn't be trusted, but that meant... I could.

Up ahead stood a large pale structure of sand and stone, or perhaps sand and bone, also encased in the never-ending stretch of white wall, the way a door sits in its frame, the front and back sliced in two, only seen on one side and not the other when closed—Yunshu's palace.

It must be difficult for the Desert Treaders to access resources in this drying heat. But knowing what stood on the other side of the walls, the stretch of water that led to Gear, made it much easier to believe they had all the necessities to survive and thrive.

The palace gates opened upon our arrival. Guards on foot and in tight sand-colored robes helped us from the Carrier.

Behind the guards stood Yunshu, and next to her was a figure half a head shorter in stature with his arms crossed—a Land Wanderer with suntanned flesh and thick hair that tumbled down to his shoulder. Both were dressed in elegant light and dark brown toned robes with gold embroidery. Jewelry adorned almost every visible body part. While Yunshu's features were smoothed down, sanded, she was still recognizable as being from Feng, whereas the Land Wanderer resembled Copper, with flesh and veins of blood peeking through the thin membranes of his skin. The pain Yunshu must have gone through to achieve such an appearance.

I wondered how Yunshu was able to survive in such a hot, dry place, and if her metamorphosis had changed not only her appearance but the construction of her biology as well.

"Lufeng." My full name sounded odd coming from someone who used to trail behind me, calling "Fengfeng."

"Yunshu," I said.

"Yena," she corrected with a stiff smile, then gestured to her partner. "My spouse, Granite. From Clay. His father used to frequently visit Feng for trade." The entire exchange was so distant, as if two strangers were meeting for the first time. I didn't think this was how family would greet one another.

"Oh, sisters!" Heshi pulled up in another Carrier. "Apologies for being late. I'd forgotten how slow Carriers are and didn't time myself properly!"

I grimaced at her enthusiasm. At least that remained the same. She was the most energetic of us all back in Feng. Most of us were on the quieter end, choosing to only speak when necessary. And more often than not, there wasn't a need to raise our voices.

"Matters not. We're all here now. Shall we?" Yunshu gestured inside her palace, and we followed.

I'd pictured this moment differently, the excitement I'd feel at our reunion, but now, with the given situation, I felt as though I was walking to my death. I wanted to speak with them alone before the dinner, but it seemed I would have to wait until it was time to leave. Or I must at least seek out Yunshu given she was the one most likely connected to the terracotta dunes in Sangshu's message.

Everything about this palace was far more decadent and elaborate than Father's, decorated with intricate patterned carpeting and wallpaper.

We entered the dining hall with our Taskers, and I found Father had already taken his seat at the table. Porcelain plates and cups with painted scroll work sat bare. Sand-colored teardrops dripped down from the cloth and brushed at our legs when we sat down at the single round table in the middle of the hall: me beside Father, Heshi next to me, then Yunshu and Granite directly across from Heshi. A seat remained empty next to Father and also one across from it.

My lingering questions about the two remaining seats were answered when the guards opened the hall doors to reveal Copper and Zinc.

In silence, they headed towards us. Copper took the seat next to Father and Zinc the seat across from her. My suspicions were confirmed when Zinc offered me a knowing smirk, expression wicked, eyes sharp, nothing like the easygoing Land Wanderer he'd first presented himself as at the market.

Copper and Zinc's entrance was calculated and timed. There was little doubt about it. My mind wandered back to Sangshu's message.

Zinc spoke first, but it still surprised me even after what I'd read in the library. "Glad for you all to gather here in celebration of a new business partner." His stare locked onto me.

Taskers came, setting down glasses and pouring wine, then withdrew.

"Before we begin—" he lifted his glass "—to Lufeng."

I mimicked the action, now mechanic and unthinking. I tried to feign surprise, to hide what I knew, and hoped it came across as shock rather than a grimace.

"I thought you were only a designer," I blurted without a second thought.

"Oh that. My deepest apologies for trying to rush things at the market. Glad I had some people keeping me in check in case I spoiled anything." He nodded his gratitude to both Tin and Copper with a lopsided smile, much to my dismay. "And designer. Well, yes," he said, both surprised and amused. "I'm a great many things, I suppose you could say. Whatever I wish to be, really." He chuckled.

Yunshu and Heshi laughed along, but I knew it was only an act.

"You have many choices when you've got *power*, Lufeng. You could have this too. Isn't that what you've always wanted?" Zinc asked. "As you all know, I've been thinking about a new palace in Glace, since the old one... well—" He took another sip of his wine. "And I think Lufeng would be the perfect fit. Don't you all think so?"

That sounded like it would bring me farther from Gear rather than closer. There were vigorous nods from Heshi and Yunshu, and Granite's nods were slow, in elegant agreement. Father and Copper simply raised their glasses.

"Do I not have a say then?" I dared.

"Oh, sweet Fengfeng." I gritted my teeth at the use of my nickname. "Don't you know by now you don't? At least not with anything on the agreement." He shook his head, then had a copy brought in by a Tasker. "Look at the top."

As I already knew, the top center of the contract was a large logo, and at the bottom was the corporation's name: Z. INC. I willed my eyes to widen in an expression of surprise. Deception had never been my strength, especially without a need for it in Feng, but it would have to be now.

"But—" I made a show of glancing at the logo on top again.

Zinc's lips twisted. He shrugged, then put his hands up. He was fooled by my performance, so far. "My father owns quite a bit. I'm just an overseer. Sometimes I like to pretend I'm someone else, see how others live—like you. Though I can't understand how anyone would want to live anywhere outside of Engine."

The air in the room tensed, but either Zinc didn't notice, or he didn't care that his words had offended everyone at the table. Copper's expression was unnaturally blank. Though upon closer inspection, why did it seem Copper and Zinc somehow resembled one another beneath the pigments brushed upon their faces? Their features—

"Your sister had such a great opportunity too, in Engine. Sangshu, was it? Poor thing. Had to resist everything we gave her." Zinc tsked. "Ungrateful, ungrateful. Now we've got bounty hunters after her. A hefty price to place her back in prison. Can't have someone so rebellious and wild running around now, can we? But *you* aren't like that, are you, Lufeng?" Zinc smiled, dropping his head forward, gazing at me through from under hooded eyelids.

It sickened me to see how to Zinc, this was all a game—life, death, none of it mattered. He saw himself as above everyone and everything, and Grandmother had once said to have such a mindset was a dangerous, dangerous thing.

"Why are you so insistent on my family?" I asked. "Why must it be us?"

"Why? *Why?*" Zinc laughed, hard. A harsh sound resembling the bark of a coyote. "Why don't you ask your *Elder*?"

I flinched at the mention of Grandmother and looked to Father. He refused my gaze.

"Guess she didn't think to tell you, huh?"

I tired of Zinc's games, but I knew the only way to win was to play, and the only way to win was to lose.

"Let my family go." I thought of Mother, of my brothers and Chuiliu. "Then I'll do anything you say."

For a moment, Zinc contemplated my proposal before

a foul smile drew his lips and brows upward. "Ah, so you've met your brothers?"

Brothers.

I blanched at his words, feeling as though winter had arrived within my body. Now it was my turn to avoid my father's stare. I kept from looking over at my sisters, should they already know about the experiments. I wouldn't be able to bear it if they were willing accomplices in Zinc's mission.

"Oh, how could you possibly think I don't know about your youngest brother? The small sapling? Within one of my own palaces?"

I clenched my teeth, feeling as though I were drenched utterly after an unannounced storm, overfilled with its waters.

"Besides," he continued, "your older brother *wants* to stay. We've become such good friends over the years. He believes in me and my work. And as for your youngest sister, I've got big plans, but you already know that."

Geming must not know about the rebellion. Surely he'd been kept in the dark about all the evil, the plotting, the true nature of the experiments. I refused to believe a sibling of mine would so willingly befriend Zinc. My belief wavered when my sisters hid from my gaze.

Zinc laughed. "If I don't let your family go, what will you do? Join that little rebellion your sister is plotting? The one I have been keeping a close eye on? The one that will surely fail any day now? Try to escape?"

Zinc seemed always one step ahead, but he could also just be prodding. It didn't mean he already knew of my plans.

"No, of course not," I retorted to his threat.

"And I've heard you've been learning how to use a Traveler. How," he offered an expression equal parts thoughtful and mocking, "diligent of you."

I tightened my grip on the sides of my chair and glanced at Tin behind me. She looked away, but rather than guilt, I saw spite, I saw envy. I would gladly let her take my place if his disgusting attention was what she sought.

"I've also heard you've had," he hummed, "a little reunion with your sister. What was her name? Chuiliu? We thought it might be safer to move her elsewhere. You know, just in case."

My mouth dried. I thought of the orbs. He knew my every move. My only choice would be to escape when he was not expecting it. But Chuiliu could be anywhere now. Inside the Palace, at another palace, maybe even on the other side of the wall already—

Or in one of the chambers. I pushed the morbid thought from my mind.

Without waiting for a response, he turned away and called for the Taskers.

The smell they carried with them, though slightly different from the ceremony, I recognized as a type of meat.

"Oh, I forgot we're having squirrel. Will that be an issue?"

I blinked, slowly, then smiled. To gain his trust, I said, "Of course not." He knew much more about me than I realized. And that was an extremely dangerous thing.

At this, Copper's blank stare faltered, a sharp glance flicking my way.

When the food was served, I took the first bite while the others seemed to await Zinc's instruction with eerie patience. They only began when Zinc raised his fork with a flourish. Though my stomach was still unsettled at first, it quickly adapted. Zinc watched each of us with amusement the entire time. I was disheartened when I noticed no one seemed to struggle with the meat. Copper watched me until both of us took the last bite of squirrel, and I wondered if she was silently mocking me in her mind the same way I was sure Zinc must be.

With the meat within me, the sensation of a rot threatening to consume me grew—creeping moss crawling within. I hoped it wasn't the squirrel I grew up with back in Feng, and if it was or even if it wasn't, I vowed to find what Zinc cared for most and tear it down, even if it was something as immense as Engine itself.

But killing, I discovered, would only be a momentary solution. Even if I took down Zinc, there would be others that could easily take his place. Sangshu seemed to have a much better plan than I did, and I had to trust Mother. Speaking to Geming didn't seem like a great idea after what Zinc had said, but maybe I could change his mind. First, I'd try to speak to Yunshu.

Zinc and Father left first after the dinner, while Yunshu, Heshi, and I stood in awkward silence while we saw them off in their Carriers.

"Shouldn't you be on your way, sister?" Yunshu glanced at the Carrier Tin and Copper were currently boarding.

"Yes, I should also be on my way." Heshi tapped her feet with impatience.

I caught Yunshu's sleeve, tugging on it the way she used to do with mine as a child. "Why did you change your names? Your faces?" I asked, quiet, drawing their attention with my bold question before they could leave me.

After a brief silence, both laughed, as if my words were ridiculous, as if they found *me* ridiculous. An earthquake rumbled within me. I wanted to cower, from Yunshu, from Heshi, from myself. But I couldn't. There was no escape from my pain.

"I have control now. I have a *say*," Yunshu said.

"You did, still do, in Feng, too," I said.

"No, sister. *You* did, but you never used it." Heshi crossed her arms. "You never took advantage of it. And now look where we are. Maybe we would've wanted to stay. Maybe we would've wanted to return."

"Don't you want our family to be whole again?" I pleaded. Did they feel nothing at all for our family or home?

"After Mother left, you knew that was no longer possible," Heshi said. "Look how happy Father is, too."

"What if she returned?" Perhaps my sisters could help me with her escape.

"It's too late." Yunshu shook her head. "Look around you. People bow down to me now. I *rule*. I no longer follow."

"Zinc rules," I whispered the harsh truth. Wrong choice, I realized, as Yunshu's expression darkened.

With desperation, I tried to draw on our childhood. "Don't you miss the fields? The bird songs? The hollows? Our home? Please, Yunshu."

Yunshu cackled, almost delirious. "*Yena*. This is my home now. This is my new family." She gestured to her spouse, who lingered by the gates of their palace. "To leave such extravagance behind, and for what? Don't be so foolish."

"But Chuiliu. Think of her. She has been given no choice. Zinc is going to experiment on her. Please. Tell me where he's moved her. Help me get her out!"

"Even if I knew where she was, I wouldn't tell you," Yunshu said. "She'll be happy here. Or wherever Zinc sends her. She'll be one of us. Isn't that what you want, sister? 'For our family to be whole again'? Why don't you join us instead of insisting on tearing us apart and away from our happiness."

No. This wasn't happiness. I wanted to tell her she

was the foolish one. But I knew now my words, my begging, had no effect on these two strangers. If not Yunshu, who was Sangshu speaking of in her message?

I released my grip on her sleeve. "Fine," I said. "With or without you, I'll bring them back. All of them. And I'll find Chuiliu, too."

Amusement lit Heshi's eyes. "This is the first time I've seen you take charge. Why didn't you do that when we were all being married off? Sacrificed? In your stead?"

I withered at my sister's words. Cold rattled down my limbs. I turned away, but I knew they didn't care. I knew Yunshu would return to her palace without a guilty thought, and Heshi to her home without hesitation. They were no sisters of mine. Not any longer.

As I returned to the Carrier, Copper's presence was suddenly glaring across from me even though she had her eyes closed. I wondered why she was returning with us, but I was shaken from my speculations as she reminded me of the copper key Geyser had given me, and I realized now it shared the same color as the Clay's terracotta dunes.

Songs of the terracotta dunes.

When we returned to the Palace, I halted Copper before she could disappear. Tin was behind us, but I waved her ahead, disappointment clawing at me now I knew she was but another of Zinc's underlings.

There was something about Copper's interactions with Zinc at the market that made it seem as though perhaps she wasn't quite on his side, and something in the way she stared at me at the dinner, exchanged glances with Aunt Xiangmu, as if to hint at her loyalties. And of course, there was Geyser's key and Sangshu's message. If I was wrong, I'd deal with the consequences later.

"Have you been watching me this whole time?" I asked in a low whisper when she turned, flicking my eyes towards the dark orbs.

She nodded so slightly, I thought I had imagined it. I kept my eyes on Tin's retreating figure in case she turned back.

I took the key Geyser had given me and slipped it into Copper's hand under my sleeve, watching for her expression. When she didn't look surprised as she took it from me, relief flooded me.

"It isn't safe for you to stay here," Copper whispered.

"When did you arrive at the Palace?" I wondered what her true connection to our family was, to Zinc, and if she was only described as an aunt because of Feng customs, and wasn't at all related to us or Father.

Her voice lowered further. "Before your father." Copper then slipped off and held up the ring made of the mixture of metal and bone. "After the contract between your grandmother and Zinc."

"My grandmother?" I asked.

"There's much you don't know about Feng," she said.

"She was the first of your people, and the only, when our grandfather found her." Copper shook her head in disbelief. "For almost four thousand years she'd been alone."

Questions about Grandmother, about the creation of Feng, weaved in my mind. She'd always said she was two centuries in age, and I'd wanted to believe her though harbored doubts about this fact. I didn't expect the reality to differ quite so much.

"Our?" I asked.

Copper paused, then said, "I'm Zinc's elder sister."

I snuck out of my room later in the night, still aware of the seeing orbs littered throughout the Palace. It was clear Tin was supportive of Zinc, yet Copper's loyalties may lie elsewhere given how she spoke of Grandmother, despite being Zinc's elder sister. With Father, I couldn't be sure. Geyser, the one I could trust most in the Palace, was nowhere to be found. Everything swam in a confusing spiral within my head as I struggled to piece together all I'd learned, unlearned, relearned since confinement within these dead halls. As I hurried down the corridor, paranoia chilled me at the thought of who might be watching me at this moment, both friend and foe.

To think everything I'd been allowed to see, along with the knowledge I'd gained, had been part of Zinc's plan—or else Copper's efforts in warning. The daunting realization both warmed and discouraged me. We were all but pawns in what now appeared to be a power struggle between siblings.

How was I to save my family while guaranteeing the safety of Feng when it seemed Zinc had the power to destroy it all within seconds? Yet, from the dinner, it seemed he needed us and our home more than he'd let on. From my findings in the library too, it seemed both Feng and Glace were the key to Engine's advancements. They needed us, more of us, and that was what the experiments seemed to be aimed at, regardless of the lives lost.

If I couldn't get Chuiliu out of wherever she was, I'd get Changqing and Mother out first before returning to find my sister. Perhaps I could rally the people of Feng to turn against the Palace once I told them about the laborers, the experiments, what was on the other side of the wall. It was nothing glorious. Not to me. But what if everyone already knew and it was only me who was unaware?

I stopped in front of Mother's door. She might not want to leave Father alone in the Palace, but the threat to Changqing could sway her. It would have to be enough. We had no time left.

"Mother," I whispered, hoping the sound would not travel through the King's door. "Mother!"

The door slid open, and right behind it, Mother was holding Changqing's hand. He'd learned how to stand, how to walk since the last time I'd seen him, progressing much faster than any sapling of Feng. But within this room, he'd never learn how to borrow the wind.

"There's no need for a goodbye," was all she said before she handed Changqing to me.

"Mother, please come with us." I reached for her hand.

She backed away, shaking her head, *no*. "There would be no room in the Traveler for me, and I don't know how to run the machine, and," Mother sighed, "I'm too frail to borrow the wind."

"There must be another way." I racked my mind for a solution. "The controller—"

Mother shook her head again. "You won't be able to get a hold of one in time."

I let my hand drop. She was right.

"I'll be back," I said. "For you and for Chuiliu."

She smiled and nodded. "I know."

I held back the choke that threatened to halt my breaths and beckoned Changqing onto my back. Confused but willing, my brother clambered on, then looked back to Mother with a questioning glance.

"I'll see you both soon," she said.

I took off in a run with Changqing bouncing against me.

When I got to the entrance, panic welled up inside me. The Travelers were not there, but the guards were.

One rushed towards me while the other kept guard by the button that would open the doors. I kicked off my shoes and tossed them to the side, borrowing what little wind I could gather around my feet, making me seem taller.

"Hold on tight," I muttered to Changqing, tensing my body to dodge the guard's grabbing hands. Even without the Traveler, and even with the wind beneath me, the guard's presence loomed above my stature, making me seem much smaller in comparison. The guard reached for my shoulder. I stepped back, pivoted to the side, and almost fell in the process.

My brother clung on, almost choking me. It was like trying to fight off two at once.

"Enough!"

We all paused. Father took long strides towards us, a menacing white shadow with his cloak billowing behind. I worried he would stop us. I feared he would bring us back to his hallway, lock us in the room with my portrait, or throw us in a chamber elsewhere in the Palace. Father didn't move towards us, but instead whirled in the direction of the nearest guard.

He grabbed their collar and, as easy as snapping a branch, whipped them backwards. Then he stormed towards the other guard by the entrance, but they fled before he reached them.

He pushed the button, and the doors began to open. Strong winds entered the Palace and pushed against our bodies, a welcoming old friend.

Father and I met eyes. He nodded, seeming to wilt at the sight of his son. I wished he would feel the urge to protect the rest of us. Or perhaps he did, but it was too late, and with Changqing, there was still a chance.

More guards appeared down the halls, rushing towards us. They must've been from the other side of the wall, released in a tsunami to consume us and hold us down until Zinc could get here.

"Go!" Father yelled as he turned to face the guards.

With raised hands, shaking, he knocked the guards back one by one, two by two, the wind trembling under his fingers. His expression exposed just how taxing it was to borrow the wind after being away from it for so long, the exhaustion quivering his limbs. Father couldn't hold on for long.

Changqing squirmed against my back, as though wanting to rush to Father's aid. I offered a soothing touch, murmuring reassurances to settle him.

I gathered more wind under my breath and felt its growing presence beneath me as I held onto Changqing and willed him to still. For the first time since I had learned how to ride on the wind, I was worried about falling.

Carried by the powerful gust, I flew, low to the ground, from the Palace gates, leaving Father behind.

"Thank you," I whispered, "Father."

12

RETURN

O nly when we passed the end of the stone path did I allow myself ragged breaths of relief.

Before I could challenge Zinc, I would first need an audience with Grandmother to learn what she knew about the origins of Feng and how it connected to Glace, Clay, the Palace, along with Gear and Engine. And I needed to know if she might be against us—if she'd been betraying her people.

I didn't know how or when I could make my way to Engine because I must find a way to save Chuiliu. Father's sacrifice might end up being for naught if I couldn't rally help from Grandmother and our people—my family.

Upon stepping back into Feng, the storm trees closed around me, their branches and leaves caressing, prodding my body, as if to ask where I'd been and who I'd become.

Out from the shadows, Grandmother stepped, and I wondered who brought her the news, whether it was the wind or the watching orbs of the Palace. Rather than greeting me with joy, she scrutinized me with a creased expression, the downward turn of her eyes and corners of her mouth. I was hoping Aunt Xiangmu might also be present, but she wasn't.

"You have to return," Grandmother said. "Go back to the Palace."

She didn't seem surprised to see Changqing on my back, nor did she ask who he was. If she already knew, that made the situation more dire. The other elders had gathered behind her to see what was causing the commotion, no doubt notified of my appearance by the wind before I even arrived. In the shadows of nearby trees, the people of Feng watched with fearful stares and unspoken whispers.

"But they are *experimenting* on our people! Not just our people, but also those of Glace. We're being used, Grandmother, for their gain, for their factories in Gear and who knows what else," I cried, hoping I could get through to her. "They still have Chuiliu. The agreement, did you know? She could *die*."

My body quaked though the earth stood still. Grandmother's expression evened. She knew everything. She knew, and she still allowed all of it to happen. The Elder standing in front of me now was not the wise protector I grew up under. She was a sacrificer, and the worst one of all.

"How can you stand still while this happens to our people?" I demanded.

"To save our people," Grandmother said, quiet.

"By killing others? By allowing them to leave?" I asked.

Never in my life had I seen Grandmother look down, but at this moment, she did.

"I'm sorry, Lufeng," she said, "but you must go back."

"No." I pushed past Grandmother, the other elders, and through the trees with blinking, watchful eyes that followed as I fled deeper into Feng with Changqing pressed tight against my back, my arms clutching onto him to both protect and to seek support.

Near the Memory Clouds, I scaled one of the tall standing trees, climbing to its peak so no one could reach me. My breaths labored with exhaustion, and I had to stop far before I reached the top to adjust Changqing's position as I could feel him slipping, to resecure him as he clung onto me using his own strength. Changqing released his hold on me once I stilled, and settled himself on a branch, clinging to the trunk.

Near us was a dark orb, and I knew who was watching.

"Come here," I said to Changqing after I calmed.

He took care to navigate the branch toward me, fearful of falling, but I brought him into my lap and curled my body around him in my sitting position. That was when I allowed the sap to run freely from my eyes.

I wanted Changqing and Chuiliu to have a choice. But everyone kept taking these choices from us all, and some so willingly accepted the path we were forced to follow. I listened to the wind and Changqing's calm breaths. This moment made me realize how much I missed home, or what I thought had been home. And the feeling of homesickness brought with it a greed, a yearning to hold onto this moment forever. But I knew I couldn't.

The gentle silence was broken by the vibration of my comscreen. Sangshu?

From my cloak, I withdrew the glass, shifting so Changqing could see it too. But instead of a message from Sangshu, flickering into view was an image of the room with the strange egg-shaped metal chambers, and standing in front of them was Zinc, along with a few guards, Geming, and—

Chuiliu.

But not only Chuiliu, Geyser too. Zinc released the chamber that held the Water Shifter, and like Geming before, Geyser tumbled out and collapsed onto the floor with blue-green liquid pooling around him, tinged in black and grey. His watery flesh was no longer clear but tainted. I thought about the articles, the low success rates of the experiments, but the reality of their failures was far worse than death alone.

I took in a sharp breath and held back a gasp.

"Always running away from your problems, so I'm told by your sisters. Will you run from her too?" Zinc's smile stretched so wide I thought his face might rip down the middle. "From him? Because he's no longer *natural*?"

"Please," I managed to say.

"Please what? Hm?" He tsked. "Didn't I warn you about taking things for granted? For rebelling? You and your family aren't great listeners it seems."

"I'll come back," I said. "Just let her go. Let her return to Feng." For helping me, Geyser suffered, but I couldn't let Chuiliu undergo the same.

"Now, now. That doesn't seem like such a great offer since you're technically supposed to remain in the Palace according to our agreement. In case you've already forgotten?" He raised a brow, dipping his head to the side.

"I'll," my mind raced with the possibilities, "I'll take her place. I'll be a part of the experiments."

"Oh, now that's an interesting proposal," he said. "But your brother. We'll need him back, too."

"Not for the experiments," I countered, clutching Changqing closer.

"You're asking for a lot, Lufeng." He threw up his hands, then dropped them, grinning. "But very well. I am a *generous* person after all."

I had no way to confirm he would keep his word, that he wouldn't throw us all into the experiments once I returned. But there was one thing I knew he would honor.

"I want a written agreement," I said.

This seemed to amuse Zinc even more because he started laughing, a sound so thunderous I thought lightning might rain down on the ceiling, shatter it to pieces.

"Very well," he said with a grand bow.

I once found his gestures chivalrous, elegant; they now seemed condescending and grotesque.

The image on the comscreen shifted, and in its place were words of Script.

"I heard you've been working very hard on your studies, so you should be able to read what it says, yes?"

"Yes," I bit back, angered by his belittling tone.

The new contract had everything my previous agreement held but with a line confirming that Chuiliu would be removed from the experiment and returned to Feng, and I would be taking her place. Though the line about Changqing was vague, stating he would simply be returning to the Palace and nothing else, I knew I had no leverage for better wording. There was another line about this being the final warning. If I were to break the contract again, the agreement would be void. And they would burn down Feng.

Was this an empty threat? Surely they still needed Feng. I thought about our numbers dwindling by the annual. Perhaps not.

"And Geyser. Let him go." I didn't know what good that would do for him now, but I didn't want them to keep his body. I hoped they'd at least allow him to return to Glace.

Zinc shrugged and added the clause to the agreement as though Geyser's life meant nothing. I stared at Geyser's unmoving form on the screen and wished I could've experienced his name in the waters of Glace, through their Song, before his death. Then tore my eyes away, refocusing on the agreement. I couldn't break down now. My family needed me.

At the end, there was a single empty line. And with a shaky writing—one neat enough to belong to someone who was born with the language yet messy enough I could recognize it as mine—I signed my name in Script.

Both Changqing and I remained silent during our descent down the tree. He returned to my back but was clinging with less urgency. Even he could feel the decreasing morale, if it hadn't already perished altogether.

We once again reached the edge of Feng, where people were still gathered, now watching our departure. Grandmother's expression was solemn, Aunt Xiangmu still unseen.

I said nothing and refused to spare her another glance as I made my way, by wind, towards where the Palace path began.

∞

At the entrance of the Palace, Zinc awaited us with his arms crossed and head tilted upward. He was still dressed in his elegant purple and white cloak but sitting with his legs dangling off the side of a Traveler. Copper was next to him in her white cloak and her face devoid of emotion. I hoped Father was safe.

"Welcome home," Zinc said.

The guards who flanked him and Copper detached themselves from their uniformed line to surround me and Changqing.

"How long did you think your little escape would last? Hm?"

"Fengfeng!" Chuiliu's voice came from behind the guards.

My hands remained clenched at my sides. "I have one request before you separate us all again," I said.

"So many requests!" Zinc said in exasperation, but nonetheless, he leaned down to listen, his face brimming with the confidence of victory and self-assuredness.

"I'd like to bring Changqing back to my mother, and to have Chuiliu meet her as well, before she returns to Feng," I said.

Past the guards, Chuiliu trembled, reaching forward towards me, but was held back by one of the many. I flung out an arm to meet her hand but just missed her fingers. I had a plan, but I needed help.

"Sure, why not," Zinc said. "You deserve some happy family time, I think. Even though you've already gone behind my back several times to get it. But don't worry. I forgive you. And this time, you have *my permission*."

I tried not to sound ungrateful in case he changed his mind. "Thank you."

"*My pleasure.*" He bowed, then gestured for me to enter the Palace.

The guard brought Chuiliu to me, and she clung onto my arm. I smiled, hoping it would calm her, but her dried sap-rimmed eyes suggested she was far past calming.

In front of us, Zinc and Copper walked. I stuck my foot out, taking a large stride, stepping on the tail of her cloak, and causing her to stumble and fall.

"I'm so sorry!" I cried as I rushed to Copper's side. Zinc snorted but kept walking as I helped her up. Before I detached myself from her side, I whispered, "Help us. Please. Bring your Traveler. And—" I choked on my next words. "Please bring Geyser home."

Copper, no doubt shocked at the risk I was taking, said nothing. Either way, I planned to leave, with or without her help. Though with her cooperation, our chances of survival would be much higher. She, too, was against Zinc, even if it was for her own secret reasons. The only question remained whether she found me worthy of the sacrifice.

When we reached Mother's room, Zinc knocked on the door, calling my mother by her name so casually it sickened me. Slowly, the door slid open, and Mother's face contracted when her eyes landed on the three of us.

"Only a few moments, not too long now." Zinc's tone was aloof, as if our family's reunion meant nothing. I wondered what had caused Zinc to become so heartless, what drove the divide between him and Copper.

We stepped in the room. Drenched in the grey light streaming from Mother's window, I remembered, below this side of the Palace was water.

13

WATER

For the first time, I felt as though my family was whole, even though we were trapped in this room with the guards and Zinc hovering outside, even though I knew not where Father now was.

When Mother looked at me, her expression fell. I flew to her side and tried to calm her with a hand on her shoulder, hoping she knew this was not the end.

She stood and waved towards Changqing. He ambled forward from behind me, wrapping his arms around Mother's leg. Then she saw Chuiliu, and sap fell, unrestrained, down her face in an unbroken stream.

"Mother." Chuiliu came forth.

Mother opened her arms and enveloped the child who barely remembered her, the child she hadn't seen age.

"You've grown up well." Mother stroked her needle threads.

It was a beautiful moment, and I wished they didn't have to reunite this way.

It seemed far too quiet outside. I only hoped Copper had decided to help and had managed to make up an excuse to leave Zinc and the guards. She could take us to Glace, or Clay—anywhere but here. Or maybe she knew how to access the other side of the Palace. There must be a secret passage of sorts. There had to be. And if she couldn't, if she didn't come—

"I asked Copper for help," I whispered, pacing towards the door to listen for any sound outside. Silence.

Mother pulled back from Chuiliu and smiled. "So you received the message."

I returned her gesture with a grin of my own. "'Trust no one, nothing, except for the songs of the terracotta dunes.'"

But my hope was waning by the second when there was a knock and Zinc's mocking voice came floating in: "Hurry it up."

There was no time left to wait. Perhaps Copper wasn't coming after all.

I had a backup plan, but it was one that might well take our lives.

"We're going to jump," I whispered, pointing to the window, then walked over to push the curtains further aside.

Mother began protest, then stopped herself.

I'd heard of Land Wanderers dying from jumping into water if the distance was too great. But for those from Feng, who were not quite as fragile, I wasn't sure what our tolerance would be. I was risking all of us, and hopefully the freedom was worth it. The swim would be far enough that we could meet death trying, but close enough that it might be possible for Chuiliu and me, having done so back in Feng when we wanted to cool ourselves in the rivers and streams. But I knew not of Changqing's familiarity with water—we'd have to take turns carrying him.

"Trust me, Mother." I was trying to convince myself more than I was trying to convince her.

I could borrow the wind to slow our landing, soften it, but it would only gather near my feet, not by my hands, not like the way Father had commanded it when Changqing and I first escaped.

"Come with us," I pleaded. Mother angled her body away, resting a hand on her chair. I didn't want us to have to separate so soon after reuniting.

"They've locked your father away, and I can't leave him." Mother fiddled with her fingers. "Take care of them, please." The look she gave all of us was one of longing. She raised a hand, caressed my cheek. "Perhaps one moon you might understand." I couldn't understand her unwavering love for Father, but hoped she was right, that one moon I would indeed understand.

"Be careful," Mother said. "Please stay safe."

I almost wanted to laugh because jumping out of the window was far from being careful or safe.

"I'll try," I managed to say through a choking sob.

With Chuiliu beside me holding my hand, and Changqing now secured to my back—we were bound together at the waist with a ripped segment of the curtains—we marched towards the window.

As I placed a foot firmly on the frame, the door slid open to reveal Zinc with a vicious, victorious smile. Guards stepped forth, casting him in an ominous shadow.

Zinc made a grand sweep of his arms, flinging them upwards. "Time's up—"

The sound of shrieking steps tore down the hallway towards the room, beckoning the heads of both Zinc and the guards to turn, along with our own.

Copper.

Then I heard the voice. "Lufeng!"

Geyser? How?

Mother, recognizing the voice, rushed to the door. I perched on the windowsill regardless.

In stampeded Geyser, half lucid, on a Traveler—Copper's. He knocked over everyone in his path, as hard as the guards tried to cling to the Traveler's legs in a futile attempt to stop its rampage. The decorative machine made the whole scene all the more spectacular as its legs bounced, creaked. Only half extended, its body and the top of Geyser's head threatened to punch through the ceiling. It flung the guards off, tossing them against the walls, causing dust to loosen and rain down from above.

"Get in! Hurry!" Geyser stammered as he lowered the Traveler.

Outside, Zinc and the guards had been knocked down. A few of them were covered in debris that had fallen from where the Traveler had fractured and damaged the walls; others were slowly rising, but still too disorientated to understand what was happening. Zinc was unconscious. And it would've been so easy to walk over and kill him with a fallen piece of the Palace he'd worked so hard to build.

Chuiliu tugged on my sleeve. "Fengfeng," she said.

I rushed towards Geyser and the Traveler, still unable to believe he was alive, and tugged Chuiliu along.

"Mother!"

She shook her head again. I wanted to run over and drag her to the machine, but a guard shook himself off and was already within a few strides of reaching her.

I left Mother for the third time and lifted Chuiliu into the Traveler first, then removed Changqing from my back and settled him in, before following.

Without a second wasted, Geyser took off. Instead of heading back towards the door, through the halls and out of the Palace, he went full speed towards the window.

"I don't know if this is waterproof or not, but here we go," Geyser shouted; the machine fluids had clearly muddled his mind as he surely wouldn't have such an outrageous idea otherwise.

"Wait, what—!?" My words slammed against the roof of my mouth as the Traveler broke through the window; its jagged edges brought with it the curtain and scraped against the frame, breaking it in the process.

As we plummeted, I clutched onto Changqing with one arm curled behind me and pulled Chuiliu closer with the other. Geyser fell back into unconsciousness. Chuiliu was shrieking, Changqing retained his usual quiet despite the danger around him, and I was stuck in my own thoughts, my cries trapped, bouncing within my mind. My arms strained with the effort of now not only having to keep Chuiliu and Changqing in the Traveler but Geyser as well.

My eyes refused to shut, unlike how everyone else's had, and I saw the water rushing towards us too quickly. I prayed in silence, calling to the wind in hope it might come to our aid, but the only wind I felt was from the rush of our descent.

I couldn't pry my eyes away until my entire body rattled, and my lids were forced shut upon our contact with the raging sea. The water around us flew upward like a cascading wall of waves before falling back down, drenching us with frigid cold that knocked the wind from my lungs in the process. We swayed and wobbled for a moment before the body of the Traveler moved to the bob of the rhythmic currents.

We were still alive, we were now safe, and we were now free.

A shaky chuckle escaped me as I stared down at Geyser. Even if he did put all our lives in danger, he also saved us.

"Sorry," Geyser muttered, half conscious now as I jabbed at the Traveler's control panel. "Good news is," I glanced around, "we're floating." Then I frowned, my fingers tapping with growing irritation. "Bad news: the controls are broken."

We searched for something to paddle with, to bring us safely to Gear before Zinc could get to us. There was nothing in the Traveler we could use.

"I didn't really have time to plan thoroughly," Geyser said, sheepish.

I shook my head, breathless. I was more than grateful already. "How are you alive?"

"Copper came for me. She said you told her to bring me home?"

I felt myself warm as I looked away.

Then, I fixed my eyes on his flesh, trying to figure out what had been mixed with his water—it was oil and something else.

"Copper can't leave. We need her stationed in the Palace. Her position of power is invaluable. Zinc knows exactly where her loyalties lie, but he can't do anything about it." Geyser's arm fell into the water. His tainted flesh leaked, mixing with the surrounding liquid. Then, a fish floated to the surface, gills unbreathing, eyes unseeing, dead. Geyser tugged his arm out of the water with a sudden alertness as he stared down at himself, as though only now realizing his current condition. Poison? Acid?

"I—" he began.

"We'll find you a healer," I said. "It'll be okay."

He looked unconvinced as he shifted away from the rest of us, covering his exposed flesh with his cloak, almost as though he feared we might become like the fish. I reached out in reassurance, but he shook his head, looking away.

"I—I won't be able to shift the water—" Geyser halted midsentence when the Traveler began to move on its own, much to all our surprise. Changqing was leaning in his seat towards Gear, hands buried up to his elbows in the water, eyes fixated on the factories in the distance. Below us, the water shifted, gently propelling the Traveler forward. Behind us, the Traveler's legs floated upward like the tail of a fish.

A Water Shifter?

We all held expressions of awe as we marveled at Changqing's ability.

He said something, but it was a garble, though it was a word similar to the Breath term for 'water.' This was the first word I'd ever heard from him.

Maybe that was why Changqing was not part of my agreement—Mother never said they wanted to use him, like Geming, as part of the experiments. Maybe he'd already been experimented on, and it was successful.

Maybe the choice Mother was speaking of giving had been the choice to choose his home, his position and role in the world, rather than the choice to be a part of the experiments.

Beneath my cloak, there was a vibration. The comscreen. I'd forgotten about it for a moment and was glad the water hadn't damaged it. The adrenaline of our escape had wiped all thoughts from my mind.

I pulled it out and Sangshu's face popped up like a floating spirit. "I'm coming," was the entirety of the message before she disappeared again.

As soon as the message finished, I threw the comscreen into the water, to Geyser's protest. If Sangshu was able to track us with the comscreen, it was likely Zinc would be able to do the same. Hopefully we would find Sangshu, or she us, before Zinc reached us. Though he already knew we were heading to Gear, he didn't know where—neither did we.

It was our fragile advantage.

I felt safe for the first time since leaving Feng, even with the currents around us threatening to throw us overboard if Changqing's concentration were to waver or break. Something looping around my neck caused me to flinch.

"You said to hold onto it until you came back." Chuiliu sat back down with a small smile.

The jade necklace I'd given her retook its place at the hollow of my collarbone. The green was brighter, more luminous, influenced by Chuiliu's health and youth. I curled my fingers around the jade, hoping she would never lose her innocence or joyful glow.

"We're okay, now?" she asked.

I nodded, and this time, it didn't feel like a lie.

Sangshu's voice echoed as the Traveler carried us towards Gear in the distance. I dared to lean against Geyser though he tried his best to move away, but when it was clear his flesh didn't seep through his cloak nor through mine, he relaxed, and I felt myself relaxing too. I held Chuiliu's hand and rested a palm on Changqing's back to steady him, as we watched the cityscape grow before us. It was colorless, dreary, with smoke drifting from the factories, fogging the skies—unalive.

But it was also hope.

ACKNOWLEDGMENTS

When I first began writing *Palace*, it had taken the form of a *Blue Beard*-esque retelling—where nature stood in as the bride and humanity as Blue Beard, and it's interesting to see just how much it has reshaped since then.

I thought about all the walls and barriers we create between one another, to contain, to confine—between humans, between species, between us and nature. I thought about the way many of us, forced or willing, step into worlds so different from our own and the jarring experience of learning customs and traditions inexistent to us previously—something that can be just as terrifying as it can be beautiful and wonderous and liberating. I hope this book has brought to you that same experience, and I hope it has helped you see past your own truths, to question, to interrogate them, and to find perhaps a different kind of understanding than the one you have always known or believe you have known.

A big thank you to all the readers who touched this book before it went out on sub: Katie, Elou, Taylor. To my supervisor at the University of Edinburgh, Patrick, for his thoughtful notes on the novella, the first half of which I turned in as part of my master's thesis in 2022. To my mentor Naben and my workshop mates Ian, Gabrielle, Maya, Jacinthe, Sunita, for their encouragement and feedback when I wrote its first chapters during the Humber School for Writers summer workshop back in 2021. To Director Jeanne from Odyssey for accepting me into the program based on the writing sample of *Palace* that was originally titled *Bone Diamond*. To my agent Lisa for always championing my chaos. And, of course, to my editor Cath, publicists Bahar and Katharine, and the entire Titan team for helping me bring *A Palace Near the Wind* into the world.

ABOUT THE AUTHOR

Ai Jiang is a Chinese-Canadian writer, Ignyte, Bram Stoker®, and Nebula Award winner, and Hugo, Astounding, Locus, Aurora, and BFSA Award finalist from Changle, Fujian currently residing in Toronto, Ontario. She is the author of *A Palace Near the Wind*, *Linghun*, and *I AM AI*. Find her at www.aijiang.ca

For more fantastic fiction, author events,
exclusive excerpts, competitions, limited editions and more

VISIT OUR WEBSITE
titanbooks.com

LIKE US ON FACEBOOK
facebook.com/titanbooks

FOLLOW US ON TWITTER AND INSTAGRAM
@TitanBooks

EMAIL US
readerfeedback@titanemail.com